The Trek to Unknown Peak

The Trek to Unknown Peak

by

V. Hanumantharao

Allied Publishers Pvt. Ltd.

NEW DELHI • MUMBAI • KOLKATA
CHENNAI • BANGALORE • HYDERABAD

ALLIED PUBLISHERS PRIVATE LIMITED

1/13-14 Asaf Ali Road, **New Delhi**–110002
Ph.: 011-23239001 • E-mail: delhi.books@alliedpublishers.com

17 Chittaranjan Avenue, **Kolkata**–700072
Ph.: 033-22129618 • E-mail: cal.books@alliedpublishers.com

15 J.N. Heredia Marg, Ballard Estate, **Mumbai**–400001
Ph.: 022-42126969 • E-mail: mumbai.books@alliedpublishers.com

No. 25/10 Commander-in-Chief Road, Ethiraj Lane (Next to Post Office)
Egmore, **Chennai**–600008
Ph.: 044-28223938 • E-mail: chennai.books@alliedpublishers.com

P.B No. 9932, No. 15, 3rd Floor (Next to Vijaya Bank), 5th Cross,
Gandhinagar, Karnataka, **Bangalore**–560009
Ph.: 080-41530285 / 22386239
• E-mail: bngl.journals@alliedpublishers.com / apsabng@airtelmail.in

Sri Jayalakshmi Nilayam, No. 3-4-510, 3rd Floor (Above More Super Market)
Barkatpura, **Hyderabad**–500027
Ph.: 040-27551811, 040-27551812 • E-mail: hyd.books@alliedpublishers.com

Website: www.alliedpublishers.com

First Reprint, 2021

Disclaimer: This book is a piece of fiction. Any similarity with respect to characters in the novel, incidents, names and places would be purely coincidental.

ISBN: 978-93-85926-05-1

Published by Sunil Sachdev and printed by Ravi Sachdev at Allied Publishers Pvt. Ltd. 1/13-14 Asaf Ali Road, New Delhi - 110002

PROLOGUE

Green Mountain is an imaginary range of mountains to the south of Himalayas. The story is about the legend of treasures atop that mountain. The stage of the drama in the novel is Green Mountain for most part and later Mumbai in the second part. As the peak of the mountain was repository of treasures, people from far and wide wished to reach that place in haste to own those riches. Aspirant people ranging from ascetics to burglars trek up the Mountain. Their interaction stage by stage unfolds the story. The ascetics believed the presence of a great spiritual master on top of the mountain and it was a life's pilgrimage for them. Some others desired to seek blessings of the Master for fulfillment of their desires. Those aspirants who didn't trust such stories however believed presence of treasures atop the mountain and trekked hard for them.

The story begins with the narration of trek of one of the groups of such aspirants to the peak of Green Mountain.

Part-I

I

There was a village called Purvasitha on the eastern side of the Green Mountain. It was close to the base of the mountain. There was little possibility for development in those parts because of the rocky and uneven terrain and the thick forest around the mountain. The business derived from the tourists to the mountain was not much as they were in a hurry to go for treasure hunting and would hardly stay in the village.

Some part of the land there was cultivable. The meager income out of the land would not provide the farmer even two square meals a day. The rest of the land was full of wild growth and trees. No amount of toil would set it right for cultivation

The sun's first rays had not emerged out yet. The fog-covered treetops were hardly visible. The village was waking up to the sounds of the cows, goats and chicks. The farmers had already left homes with their oxen to work in the fields.

On the way to the mountain and at some distance from the village, there was a tea-shop. It was made of thatched roof and earth and stone walls. The front portion of the tea-shop had an extension of portico like thatched structure. This facility helped those who prefer to drink tea standing outside while savoring the beautiful ambience. At the back of the shop there was a small raised platform of stone slab where they brew tea and make snacks on a kerosene stove. A teen aged boy in soiled half-pants and shirt was busy with tea kettle on the stove. He looks up at the visitors now and then for orders.

Those who plan a visit to the mountain would have nothing to do with the village. Whatever they need for the trip, they bring with them from their places. They knew that they would not get anything required for the trip, from that village.

So they reach the tea-shop situated on the outskirts of the village from where they begin their trek. Of course there were other routes to reach the base of the mountain as well.

Two visitors of middle age, sitting in the tea-shop on a rough wooden bench enjoyed the hot morning tea. There was no other furniture in the shop, but for those wooden benches and equal number of tables in front of them, to keep the tea cups and snacks plates.

The visitors appeared strangers to that place. Their language and dresses were different from the locals. They were in tight pyjamas and white loose shirts. They had white turbans and black shoes.

"Is this the way to the mountain?" one of the visitors asked the shopkeeper, while keeping down the teacup on the table before him. He brushed off the traces of tea on his moustache with the back of his hand.

"Yes" the shopkeeper answered. He came across many such visitors in his decade old business.

"Treasure hunting?" he queried after a while, with a glint of mockery in his eyes. He was adjusting his soiled turban for no reason, as was his wont.

The visitors did not like the fun from a stranger. He might talk like that with the villagers, or those who were familiar with him but not with newcomers.

One of the two, Nanda resenting the sarcasm replied "That's none of your business." He was clean shaven and looked urbane. He was taller than his companion.

The chastened shopkeeper to make amends said "Look there beyond those trees, that is the way to go up." He pointed out the way to the mountain. The visitors turned their heads thither, while shading their eyes from the hurting sunrays falling in through the window. The sun was rising up, warming the surroundings. What the shopkeeper showed them was a strip of clearing in the dense forest on a rising rocky land.

The shopkeeper continued "Of course, there are other routes too. But this is the shortest one. In total there are five camps. After that one reaches the top of the mountain, the place of the legendary treasures. You could break the trek at those camps for rest and food. Of course, you have to stop for the night stay perforce at one of the camps, on your trek."

The second of the visitors, Brahma, while smoothing the unruly hairs of his moustache, asked him "Can we get any help on the way?"

Shopkeeper replied "You will find visitors on the way. They could be of help to you."

While they were talking, another person stepped in. He sat beside the visitors, facing the shopkeeper, with his legs dangling. He appeared familiar to the shopkeeper. The bench could accommodate three customers easily. The empty tea cups were on the table in front of the visitors.

The newcomer who was a guide heard them talking about the journey and said eagerly "I will take you there, if you need any help." He heard them while he was enjoying his first cigarette of the day standing outside. The shopkeeper did not like the cigarette smoke and would not allow smoking inside.

"Are you a guide?" Nanda asked not even looking at him. He wanted to preempt the possible high rate for the service, by appearing to be casual.

The guide whose name was Balu replied "Yes, I charge two hundred rupees per day for one person and food and drink are extra."

Balu was a young man of thirty, stout and of a jovial disposition. He wore pants and shirt, which were crumpled though washed clean. There were no facilities for ironing there and the village folk though studied in schools would not find it necessary. He had old black shoes on his feet.

Balu began slurping tea, which was brought to him just then by the tea-maker boy who returned to his place at the back of the shop in no time.

"Where do we get food? We have no arrangements even for our food." Brahma said.

Nanda thought that the guide was taking advantage of his monopoly.

"We don't need you; it is a waste of money. We can manage ourselves. There will be other visitors to help us in case of necessity." He said.

The shopkeeper interjected now "But you know, after some distance on the way you come across a forest. There are wild animals. You need to be careful in trekking and a guide will be of help to you certainly."

Nanda did not like his interference. The shopkeeper too was taking advantage of the situation, he thought.

He said irritated "Are you frightening us?"

Brahma placating his companion said "Let's employ him up to some distance. Of course, if only he makes the rate reasonable."

He asked Balu for a reduction in the rate.

The guide Balu thought over for a moment. Then he settled for fifty less. He considered instead of losing this pair of visitors, getting fifty less would be better. That would take care of his expenses for two days. He also remembered his competitor Subbu who would not lose even a single visitor. He fought with him many times for undercutting the rates.

The guide asked them "Are you well prepared for the long journey?"

"Yes, we brought things we need on the journey, as far as we guessed." Brahma said.

"Do you have a torch light and some medicines used for common ailments?"

"Yes, we brought them."

They got food packed for three, from the shop. The visitors paid the shopkeeper and then they were on their way, with the guide in the lead. They had bulky bags slung over their shoulders. The preparation was for more than two weeks, with no chance of replenishing the supplies on the way. The entire region of trek was forest area and uninhabited, but for the ashrams also called camps, providing food and shelter at some places.

The trees at that place were not tall and were near to each other leaving very little place to walk between them. The trek was made possible by the path formed by the villagers who go up the mountain to get fuel and fodder for their cows and goats. On either side of the pathway small plants and thick vegetation thrived.

It had become warm now, with the bright sun up in the sky. But the cool breeze grazing the green leaves touched them, making the walk pleasant. They heard voices of some others at close quarters. Many others were on trek with the same purpose. However, the small trees and foliage impaired their visibility.

Nearby, there was a ruffle in the grass when a fox chased a terrified rabbit. The presence of humans did not deter their pursuit of instincts of necessity.

Balu pulled out a cigarette pack from his shirt pocket. He lighted one and sucked the smoke in a long pull, with the joy reflecting on his large face.

The guide asked the other two "You belong to which place?"

Nanda did not like the other's curiosity about their personal matters.

He asked the guide with irritation "Is it necessary for you to know such details?"

Balu with a smile replied "There is no harm in knowing each other. If we talk to each other, we could lessen our boredom as well as strain."

Brahma answered "We hail from southern parts. We heard people discussing about the treasures in the mountains since many years. In fact, whenever the villagers talk of money making, they refer invariably to these mountains."

"Did anybody near your town return with success from the trip?" the guide asked.

"We heard some tales about that. But we haven't met anybody who reached the top." Brahma said.

Nanda replied "Yes, there are many interesting stories about these mountains since ages."

Brahma asked the guide "That's all right. How far you went, did you visit the top?"

He wanted to know the depth of knowledge of the guide about the mountain.

Meanwhile, inspired with talk of treasures, Nanda asked the guide with enthusiasm "That apart, can we reach the first camp today?"

The guide throwing the cigarette butt away, "I have not gone that far. Regarding reaching the first camp; not so fast, you may reach the first camp by tomorrow at this rate. Of course, your shoes are good for hill climbing. You are well advised on that score. But this pace of trekking is hardly enough. You are new to this hill climbing. I mean you don't have the practice."

"I agree, but after a few days we could pick up speed with the experience gained." Nanda replied.

His enthusiasm about the trip had doubled with the conversation about the treasures atop the mountain.

"May be you are right, but not before reaching one or two camps. To start with, you must cultivate discipline. You need to change your food habits. You must resort to single minded effort." Balu said.

Annoyed at the sermons, Nanda threw away the half-eaten banana hitting the trunk of a tree by the side. He had been displaying his short temper often even in those trying circumstances. Brahma shook his head in disapproval.

"Where did you learn all this glib talk?" Brahma said to the guide with laughter.

"Don't under estimate my advice. I am in this business since many years." The guide said with a gesture of warning.

He continued "Some months back, I saw a couple. They could reach the second camp in three days. On the second day after that, they reached the third camp."

Brahma asked "After that? Did they reach the top?"

"I learnt from my friends that the husband only was seen at the higher camps." The guide said with a smile.

"What happened to his wife? Did you accompany them by any chance?" Nanda jibed at the latter with a suppressed smile.

Brahma laughed at this query.

The guide did not like that, but replied without irritation "They said she disappeared on one of the nights. But her husband did not mind that. He endured the separation and proceeded further. Such persons only will succeed."

He said this with a benevolent smile, which appeared comical. The visitors looked each other and laughed for the sermons given by the guide.

Nanda asked him, "Did she go away on her own or something happened to her?"

Balu did not answer.

He bent and then broke the branches of the small trees on either side of the narrow path to make way for them.

"I think she used the good opportunity to get rid of an unwanted husband." Nanda made his flippant comment.

Brahma asked Balu, with a smile "You mean to say, we have to sacrifice our partners to get to the treasures?"

The guide gave no reply.

After a while he said "We must walk fast. By evening we must reach some place of rest."

After some time, Nanda asked him, "By undertaking all this trouble, what kind of treasure one can expect there?"

"They say there are heaps of gold, silver and other valuables, for the benefit of the lucky few. It seems some people stored those treasures there, after toiling for many decades. It is said that, it's impossible to evaluate them." The guide said.

"After reaching the top, they must be fighting each other over the treasures." Brahma opined.

Nanda now convinced of the hardship in reaching the peak said "My friend, it's not easy for anybody to wish and take them away. The hardship itself is the deterrent for lesser people."

He was positive of the availability of the treasures and wanted to assure himself of their safety till they reach them.

He then addressing the guide, "You are here since many years, did you come across anyone returning with treasures from the mountain top?"

The guide laughed scornfully and said "What a slick query? Do you think anybody with treasures come to you to show it? Will he reach home safe after that? We have to assess that from his later life style."

"That's right. No sane person will disclose such matters, I agree. But have you seen anyone, whose later life style was changed, I mean after the trip to the mountain?" asked Brahma.

The guide did not reply. He bent his head as if to avoid any more talk on that. Then pulled out a cigarette and lighted it.

He asked after a puff at the cigarette, "Do you have any weapons, to be used in case of necessity?"

"What weapons? Are we going to fight somebody on the way?" Nanda asked with a sneer.

"I have a pen knife." Brahma readily answered. He understood the relevance of the query. They may come cross some wild animals or even some other visitors may create trouble for them.

Nanda now said, "I have my walking stick. It was good for warding off street dogs. I could use it now."

He took the query of the guide as a joke.

The guide laughed loudly and then said soberly "Anyway, that's my observation and advice to you. You certainly need some weapon for self-defense."

The path, though it was a hill track was not difficult to trek. The rocky terrain covered around with soft soil was not hurting to walk. The track there was almost like level ground and it was easy for trekking.

By evening, they reached an extensive level ground, where they saw eating places and accommodation for night's stay. Those shelters were made of thatched roofs, sloped to one side with walls of wood rafters and leaves closely knit. It was in two parts, one for cooking and taking food and the other longer one for sleeping in the night.

They ate the snacks offered by the keeper of the inn. They ate rotis and vegetable curry. "The snacks are as good as eating at home. If we get food like this, trekking becomes easier than what we imagined." Nanda said.

"But you would not be lucky all through to get such tasty food. And some days you may not get anything; you must be prepared for that. My advice is, you always try to carry some eatables, wherever available for next day." Balu's sensible advice was that.

Mats made of wild grass were provided to lie down on, in the verandah. The visitors spread bed sheets which they brought with them on the mats to make them more comfortable. The verandah was secured with screens made of sticks on all the four sides and for a door on one side. The thatched screens provided shelter from cold and wild animals to the possible extent.

There were many others besides the guide and his companions, who occupied the place in the verandah. Though they were less than a score of people, they represented the length and breadth of the land. Some strange looking persons too shared the shelter. They wore a variety of clothing, some known and some other types not known to a section of the visitors.

Next to Balu's group, three young persons with a rustic appearance huddled together in a human ball. They looked around with fear and uncertainty lest somebody might throw them out anytime. They appeared desolate and took the direction of the mountain as a last resort. They had no chance for making preparations needed for the trek and the difficulties to face. They had no bags and were bare footed. They shivered in the cold and huddled together to ward off the discomfort to some extent.

Balu suspiciously looking at the ball of youngsters asked addressing none in particular "Who are you? And where do you think you are heading?"

The ball now split into two. The smaller one appearing to be bolder than the other larger spoke hesitantly "I am Ramsaran. These two are from my village only."

His eyes were bright and steady, though he was shaky.

Brahma smiled to give him confidence and asked, "But why are you going away from your village?"

"We don't want to be killed there. Very few could survive the cross-killing in those parts. Some families were completely wiped out in mass destruction."

Brahma asked "What is the cross killing for?"

"The village which is situated on the border of Bihar and Chhattisgarh was very backward and close to the forests. Naxalites infested those areas. The poor villagers were influenced by their gullible talk. Many young people joined their cadres for a small wage, which helped their starving families.

But the police raid the villages in search of Naxalites. They target first the families of the villagers who joined the cadres. The police harass them to find out the whereabouts of the Naxalites. The terror-stricken family members fled their villages to the towns nearby, leaving things as they were in their homes. In towns they were exploited by the middlemen and became cheap labor. And the women were helplessly turned into lust satisfying flesh pots to anybody who could acquire them by force or by paying money to the middlemen."

Nanda listened to him in surprise and asked "You appear to be knowledgeable. Did you study in school?"

"Yes, I studied in school. I learnt more from the village life and society. I used to read books borrowed from others. I read about Chairman Mao, who was responsible for Maoism, the principle of power flowing thro' the barrel of the gun and the consequent massacres, Kanu Sanyal and his adaptation of the 'Maoism' and so on. But I think the power flowed thro' the barrel of the gun alright, but the barrel was bent backwards, towards the people who were around the holder of the gun. We suffered the gun fire."

"What about those who held the gun?" Brahma asked him.

Ramsaran replied "Their families are well provided for, I think. Their leaders have the required means."

Nanda said "I heard they and their progeny are well taken care of. Public are afraid of them and money was no problem. Any movement unless, it is taken up after briefing to the people and acceptance by them would not last. Sufficient groundwork should be done in advance. The groundwork is service. It would take decades for the groundwork to show results. The voices of such organizers are the guns and their words are the bullets. They bring out the flowers of the results for everyone to see."

He read much literature on that topic.

"The violence unleashed by the police on one side and the retaliation by naxals on the people who they think had informed the police, are the barrels of the guns aimed at the people, who are supposed to be benefited by the movement. But whatever had happened led to the blood bath. At one time, it is naxals who have the upper hand and another time the police as in some southern states. But the movement cannot sustain a permanent progress without the parti-cipation at the grass root level. The sufferings of the people persist till some solution is found. So what do you think is the duty of the government in this regard?" Nanda continued.

"I don't say that the problem can be solved only by government. They must enlist the services of the other service agencies. We are coming across a number of financial scams every year, accounting to the tune of millions of rupees. I read in newspapers. A part of the money recovered could be utilized for the uplift of the masses, if at all it is recovered as reported in the media. Tax evasion and corruption are other areas to be controlled and the monies recovered could be utilized for the cause of the people." Ramsaran replied.

"What is important is the mentality of the people at the helm of affairs. As long as they are of low morals, the benefits would never reach the people. So there could be local committees who should be entrusted with development works. Avoid the big contractors for small works. There are many unemployed youths in the villages. They would work with sincerity. Young men and women are better placed in combating the menace of corruption" said Brahma.

"That could be an experiment worth trying," replied Ramsaran.

"But why did you flee from your village when you have many ideas for betterment? You could have waited and worked with your people."

"That is my long term aim. Our flight to the Green Mountain is for two reasons. One is the escape from the imminent warring groups so that we return at a better time. The second one is that we could explore the treasures that could be utilized for the people."

Brahma said, "That's right. I appreciate your sense of priorities and timing."

"I wish you success and luck." Nanda said while stretching himself down on the mats.

The tired visitors slipped into slumber one by one, recollecting the comforts of life they missed because of the adventure they undertook now. Ramsaran and his friends lied down in one corner with regained confidence by the support of those visitors. Somewhere nearby villagers were singing tribal tunes which reached the visitors in low vibrations.

II

Early dawn, noises made by birds and goats were reverberating in the surroundings.

The visitors were busy in attending to calls of nature. They were getting ready for resuming the journey.

Tea was prepared with goat's milk there. One rarely came across buffalos and cows at that altitude. The reason could be the bulky bodies of those animals. Secondly, sufficient demand was not there for the large quantity of milk they yield, as the visitors were not that many. They were sipping tea served in earthen cups. Outside the hutments where they slept the previous night, long rock formations served the purpose of benches for sitting. A few other visitors too were there for the tea session.

The surface of the ground appeared green, covered with grass. Small smooth stones peeped through the greenery.

A stranger in dhoti and long shirt, aged around forty joined them. He carried a bulging backpack, though appeared to be on a casual hike. Other visitors stared at him with surprise for his unusual dress and also as he came alone for the trek. He was not in a group like others who trekked the mountains.

The guide asked him, without losing time. He could be a potential customer.

"Sir, from where you are coming?"

The stranger, "I came from the western side" and he queried the guide, "How are you?"

The guide was surprised and asked him, "Did you see me before?"

"Yes, you are Balu the guide. I came here before. I came twice."

Nanda asked him without sticking to any formality as is his nature, "Who are you, sir?"

"I am Charudas. That is my pen name. I wrote books with that name. I secured awards a number of times. You must have heard my name."

"Yes, it sounds familiar. My name is Brahma. Are you too after the treasures?" Brahma said.

"I guess his earnings are not much now. Or this may be a better and easier option." Nanda opined.

"None, that life had lost its charm. Of course I also needed some new ideas."

Nanda laughing and addressing his companion "Brahma, you heard him? He is going to the mountains for nothing, leaving aside so much money and name as a writer."

"There is not that much money as you imagine in this business of writing. Anyway do you think money and name are the only things in life? Should not there be some adventure?" Charudas said.

Brahma switching to the subject of writing "Before starting to write, do you make a sketch?"

He appeared to be more interested than others in writing. He might be having some fancy about writing stories. Or it was only to pass time in those remote surroundings. But Charudas was sincere and clear in describing his idea of writing.

"You need to have imagination. It is like a horse to a carriage. Knowledge is the driver. Language is the carriage. The subject on which you chose to write is the path or highway."

"Are you to be armed with so many things to write? That is right. I agree it is a gift of God. Then getting recognition and money depends on one's own capability and fate."

Balu the guide, getting up from his seat, "Shall we start now?"

Other two visitors picked up their bags and followed him.

Charudas too got up and followed them with his bag.

"I too would come with you some distance if you don't mind"

"You know guide charges are two hundred per day or part of the day." Balu's quick response.

Charudas smiled and said "Alright, I would pay you that. I could reduce my tiredness, if we walk in a group."

Balu opined, "We reach the destination fast."

Others laughed.

The surroundings were pleasant up to some distance, due to the soft green grass underneath as also the close-knit leaves of the trees overhead like an umbrella.

"I believe the visitors to this place are greedy. I detest their all engulfing desire for the treasures. Or else, they must have been disappointed with life and come here desperate to achieve something," Charudas observed.

"Why should you judge like that? I have come here for adventure and treasure hunting is only a second option. I am not disappointed with my life either. I will continue with my business after this trip," said Brahma.

Nanda to tease him, commented "Unless you put in a wholehearted effort, you cannot succeed in any venture, leave alone Green Mountain."

"Let's see. Anyway this thrill of adventure itself is great."

"You can jot down your experiences of this trip and make a travelogue."

Nanda exclaimed "Aha! Now I know why you are on this trip a second time."

"You are right to a great extent. Moreover, I do not have any urgent responsibilities to discharge at home," Charudas said.

Balu the guide "Sir, for success in this treasure hunting, one must have another quality."

"What is that?" asked Brahma.

"One should possess steadiness and sincerity of purpose, they say."

Brahma said "For success in any activity steadiness and sincerity are necessary. But in this case, nobody for certain, can say he had seen a person who secured anything of the treasure or even talked to such a person."

"That's right. It's like the existence of God," said Charudas.

* * *

Sun reached the zenith. They felt the heat now. The number of trees giving them cover too dwindled. After some time, they found themselves at a vacant place under a large tree. There were no obstructing rock formations or wild bushes there. They must be wary of snakes and scorpions and such creatures which inhabit beneath rocks or in bushes. Balu broke a branch of a tree and used it to clean the place. Brahma followed suite. Then they all settled down under the tree.

After opening the bags, they pulled out the packets of food brought with them and began eating hungrily. They were tired and hungry. As they were told water would be available on the way, they had not brought any water bottles with them. Guide Balu informed them of a lake nearby. They walked towards the lake.

The flowing water from the nearby waterfalls formed that lake. There were small water streams and larger waterfalls. The waterfalls appeared at a distance where the rock formations were steep and ended in a valley. The water there was crystal-clear. One could see the round shaped stones of different colors underneath. Small fish swam across hither thither freely in the shallow water. They ran helter-skelter fast sensing the footsteps of the visitors.

The leaves of branches of the trees on the bank were close to the water surface in the lake. When the wind forced them, the branches rose up carrying droplets of water with them, and sprayed on the grass that adorned the bank.

The place where the water was flowing into the lake, the distant waterfalls and fantastic rock formations and so on enchanted Charudas, the writer.

Charudas commented that he missed all those beautiful spots during his last visit to the mountain.

At a distance, water born birds had a great fun on water, while feasting on the abundant fish available there.

A cool breeze blew suddenly from where the water was falling down to the ground from the hills. The foul odor it brought was unbearable and unusual.

The birds on the trees and the wild animals moving peacefully at a distance from the visitors till then began howling frantically as if something scared them now and moved away fast.

Guide Balu became rigid with fear. He turned his gaze hesitantly towards the waterfalls. He saw expectantly the striped beast through the wild grass and low branches of the trees.

Balu cautioned his companions in under tone, "Look there, it's a tiger moving towards the water. Of course, we have nothing to fear as the breeze is blowing now towards us. So it cannot smell us. Moreover, it would not venture into this marshy land, this far and it is far off, at least half a mile away."

They finished the chores of washing faces and hands and after gulping water, walked back hurriedly to the tree under which they ate a short while ago.

They rested there after making sure from Balu once more, that tigers would not come that far.

Brahma looking at Charudas asked him hesitantly, "Sir, are you married?" and after some time he added, "I think you don't mind my personal enquiries."

"No... no. I don't mind at all. I am sufficiently advanced in age for that. I am married and we have a son. My wife and son live at my place. As I go on tours, that too on long tours sometimes, they stay there. My son is studying in high school. My wife works as a teacher in the same town."

"I am surprised at the cooperation extended by your family to you, though you are away from them frequently." Nanda opined.

"My old mother resides with them. My wife takes care of her too. Not many housewives are like her."

"If you get sufficient treasure atop this mountain, it would solve your problems of touring," Brahma interjected.

"May be you are right."

"What about your efforts of collecting materials on this trip, for writing a book?" Nanda asked.

"Of course, that is also there. That is always there, irrespective of the treasures or no treasures."

"Is that desire to write is so irresistible?" Nanda asked.

"In a way it is so. Something in you urges to write. It does not depend on your desire for fame or money. If incidentally you get them, it is alright. It adds some satisfaction."

"But how strong is the desire? Because you said incentives are not the motive force. But disincentives like say, if somebody forces you not to write or circumstances do not cooperate your writing. What you do then?" that was Brahma's query.

"Yes, incentive or no, even disincentives would not stop a writer, when he wants to write. You might have heard about Salman Rushdie and cases of other noted writers who were outcast and persecuted. You also know the case of the lady writer who left her country, Bangladesh in this connection. But they have not changed their opinions or abandoned their work. As somebody said it is the combined work of writer and God. It is the gift of God."

A group of birds landed on the upper branches of the tree with chirping and fluttering of wings.

Balu woke up with the disturbance.

He got up and said, "Enough of the rest. Let us start on the trek again."

"Where is the hurry? Wait for sometime more. It is nice to sleep here." Nanda said while yawning.

"You have seen the tiger. It is safer to reach some village before dark." Balu struck the warning note.

With that warning they jumped into action at once.

III

By morning of third day, Brahma and Nanda paid Balu the amount due and sent him away. They considered him not necessary any more as they became familiar with the daily life of a trekker.

Charudas was not seen around now. He left them the previous day.

Nanda and Brahma resumed their journey. As they reached higher altitudes, the sun was not so hot now.

At a distance ahead of them, they saw a man and woman. After a few minutes, they reached them. The woman was aged thirty plus and attractive. Her husband appeared ten years older to her. They must be hailing from north, Nanda guessed. The husband wore pants and shirt. His wife was in loose shirt and pyjamas. Both had leather boots with upturned flaps for protection against cold and injuries due to sharp stones. They might protect them against snake bites too, to some extent.

Brahma asked the strangers in hindi, "Are you heading for the last camp?"

The new person identified himself as Veera and his wife Chandra.

He replied, "I think so, if we can."

The woman interposed and said with a tired dry smile "Before starting on this journey, we planned like that. But the present situation is different and not so conducive."

Nanda said sympathetically "Yes lady, it's a tedious journey. For women, it's more so."

Her husband did not agree with that and said "I think it is immaterial if the visitor is male or female. The facilities and obstacles are the same for both. I think there are no special safe guards for men when attacked by a wild animal or a dacoit."

Nanda ogling the woman "Anyway, the case with women is different. We go about, as we like. We eat and sleep anywhere. Women cannot simply do that way."

Others did not comment.

They reached a place by midday, where they saw some arrangements for food and rest. As usual hutments were there and visitors thronged to the place. Odors of freshly cooked food items wafted around.

Nanda and Brahma and some others ate in the non-vegetarian enclosure. Veera, Chandra and others had meals in the vegetarian section. Food was served in leaves like that of Banana plants, spread on floor neatly smoothened. It appeared like cemented surface. There were many other visitors waiting for food at that place. Some were washing their hands and feet. A few others were busy in partaking food. Many others sat under the trees for rest. Unless the visitors took advantage of the resting places wherever they were available on the way, they would suffer later for lack of food and rest.

After taking food, Nanda commented, "Meals tasted very good. I had never tasted such."

An old man sitting by his side said "They blend meats of different animals in the preparation of meal here."

"What do you mean?"

The former, "After cooking they mix different types of meat before adding other ingredients. We do not know what else they do. Many kinds of animals live around this place, you know."

"That may be true. They must be cooking in an ingenious way. But food is good. I would be glad to stay here for a day or two."

Brahma looked at him in surprise.

"We haven't reached the second camp as yet. It appears already we are forgetting the purpose of our journey." He said as if uttering to himself.

"What's the urgency now? The treasures won't be depleted so fast." Nanda uttered yawning.

Nobody said anything.

After some time, refreshed up, they were on their feet again. Many others joined them.

Nanda and some other visitors were still sleeping. Brahma got up and joined others who were on the move.

Chandra and Veera were in the lead. Brahma looked back a few times for his companion. However, Nanda did not follow them.

They felt the walk easier now.

Veera said, "As we go up, the trekking becomes easy. It is said that facilities are more—free facilities."

Chandra appeared satisfied now, after the initial tough journey. She walked close to her husband.

Brahma said, "But at higher altitudes, it should be difficult to climb due to lack of oxygen."

"That's unique about this journey. It might be because of the type of trees around here." Veera said.

"How do you know?"

Veera replied with a smile, "We met a saint on the way, he said."

In fact he guessed so.

After walking for a number hours, they felt tired. They rested under a tree. Because of the breeze the place underneath the tree became clean, saving them the trouble.

Then they saw Nanda and some others walking towards them, at a distance. Amongst them Ramsaran and his two companions were there. They have shed their timidity by now. Nanda was laughing happily while talking with them. They became good companions.

Brahma jeered him "I knew, you cannot travel without my guidance."

Nanda smiled and said "Don't show off. I could not stay, as nobody was there to give company to me."

"What about Ramsaran?"

"He joined me with his friends on the way."

Those who felt the need went behind trees at a distance and eased. The women folk had to walk on the other side and went behind a large rock formation. Within minutes, there was a shriek from one of them. Two of the men resting under the tree ran there, to find a green snake that fell from the adjoining tree. One of the men killed it with a large stone lying there. The two men then returned with gratified male pride. The women leisurely joined the group after finishing their job.

Nanda laughed and commented loudly, "I said for women these journeys are cumbersome. This is the reason."

Single men of the group joined the laughter.

After a while, the visitors began their trek once more.

Few hours later at some distance, they saw a number of shacks made of wooden rafters and broad leaves of some trees.

It was getting dark. Lights with different luminosities shone through the windows and open doors in some places.

After going near them, they found them to be places of residence for the visitors to the mountain. We might call them ashrams because that term fits the structure and purpose of those shelters. They were given to understand that mendicants stay for their spiritual pursuits. But they were free of any such persons at that time. So the visitors to the mountain could use them.

Veera and Chandra found place in one of the rooms. Brahma went into another as Nanda wanted separate accommodation. Those who maintained the ashram gave to understand that single visitors could take the help of persons serving in the ashram. They were charming and helpful to the visitors, in reducing their tiredness. One of those women served Brahma and another helped Nanda. Those women were familiar with herbal medicines and the visitors were benefited by those potions and ointments. Of the other visitors, some preferred to be alone. Ramsaran and his friends were huddled together on the mats provided by the ashram-people in the hall.

* * *

When the visitors woke up early dawn next day, they were surprised and pleased beyond limits to watch the exceptionally beautiful surroundings of that place. Grass with small colorful flowers covered the ground like a carpet. The trees were moderately tall with broad leaves. Shining mist settled on the leaves. Some other trees were with ripened fruits of varied types.

"I don't know when we could reach the second camp." Veera said.

An aged man by his side clarified, "This is the second camp. There won't be name boards fixed indicating the numbers of the camps, you know."

Brahma pleased with progress made, said "That is a good progress. There would not be any problem if I stay here one more day."

Nanda commended the observation of Brahma.

"Now that I have company, I too would stay back." He said.

Veera looked at them in disbelief, at the change in their nature brought over by the charms on the way. Chandra turned her head away trying to suppress a smile.

The visitors ate fruits for breakfast and were on their trek again. Ramsaran and friends followed Veera at a distance. They appeared not tired; they were accustomed to walk on rough roads and hill tracks. The soiled pants and shirts they wore gave very little protection against the cold breeze. They wore leather sandals as the villagers do, obviously lent by someone on the way.

Melted snow in a small drizzle began falling on them. As it was not making them wet, they felt the walk pleasant and moved on. The snow evaporated once it was on their bodies.

After some time, however, it became a trickle of larger drops. They all ran to the shelter of a huge tree. Already some people were under it.

When the rain subsided, the long walk continued again.

Veera looked at the person who was close behind him. He was a young man of thirty years. He was not talking to anyone and introverted. He appeared weighed down by sorrowful thoughts.

Veera asked him, to help lessen his burden of thoughts, "You are coming from which place?"

The young man replied, "I am Nishit. I come from the eastern city of Rudrapura."

He became silent and lost in his thoughts again.

Suddenly Veera heard a familiar voice behind him.

"You are old. How could you undertake the hard trek?"

That was Charudas.

The old man replied with a carefree smile, which showed a gap of three front teeth, "I will trek to the extent I can."

He continued with sarcasm, "Don't bother I would not come in your way for grabbing the treasures."

Chandra commented, "If he gets the treasures he can live happily for the rest of his life. Money brings back youth and vigor too"

She smiled looking towards her husband.

Another visitor, a young man walking close to them said "And money can bring back the teeth he lost too, I think."

They all laughed, but for the old man.

Veera addressing Charudas, "When did you join us? We missed you these two days."

"I was stuck up there at the previous camp, as I was engrossed in writing."

They walked fast as the conversation helped to forget the tiredness. Unusually the ground was not marshy, even after the rainfall.

"Even after such a long drizzle, the ground is not wet and slippery, saving us the trouble." Chandra was happy for that. She changed into a sari now.

Concurring with her, the young man behind them known by now as Sharad said, "Yes, it's not slippery like the wet ground."

Charudas said, "Water has dripped away to lower levels. Moreover, the land here is full of gravel. It's like smoothened floor."

"Yes, that's true in some places the ground is shining like mosaic floor," said Chandra.

"Anyway our trekking has become easy, in spite of the rain." said Veera.

Addressing Charudas he asked "Are we nearing the next camp, I mean camp three?"

"That depends on the pace of our walk, if not today, tomorrow."

Chandra holding up the pink and blue sari folds away from the ground said, "Yes, if not today, tomorrow we will reach the camp. It's tiring to climb the hill, now steeper than before."

The round symmetric legs of the lady drew the eyes of the young Sharad to them, like the wild bee to the fragrance of a flower. She at once dropped the sari down.

Sharad commented with a contented smile, "Probably this trek is not suited for ladies."

The sky was clear and the cold breeze was pleasant. The pilgrims were climbing up happily. Everyone had only one aim in mind—to go up further and further—that too as fast as possible and as comfortably as the circumstances permit.

The green grass on both sides of the path looked like thick carpet. The thin dew remained on the small blades of the grass. Strange flowers on the grass appeared as those grown in parks. Not far away, trees of not much height and names unknown swayed hither thither in the light breeze.

Charudas intoxicated with the heavenly sights, "I never guessed that nature could be so enchanting."

Veera smiling, "Yes, I too never saw such beautiful sights in my life before."

Sharad with a mischievous smile said to Charudas "This trek is difficult for ladies, as I said. But as a writer you may appreciate that without ladies around us we may not enjoy the beautiful nature well."

"Of course, they will add to the completeness of the scenic beauty." Charudas quipped absent-mindedly.

After a while he asked Sharad, "You are quite young for this trek, though your opinions appear knowledgeable."

Charudas did not like the other's comments about ladies and his writing. Sharad was not old enough for that.

He wanted to find out the other's motive of the trip, by that indirect comment.

But Sharad understood and he said, "I am a sportsman. I climbed a few mountains, of course not very famous ones. I am in the practice now."

"But do you know this mountain is famed for the treasures atop it?"

"I heard that. But I don't know how far I go. That depends upon my moods." He smiled and continued "I am a moody man. Of course I like good things of life." He pulled out from his front pocket, a small flask of wine and had a quick swig, while ogling unabashedly at Chandra, the lone woman in the group.

At some distance ahead of them, a few people were walking very fast.

Veera in a lighter vein said, "They are walking so fast as if to become the very first to lay their hands on the treasures."

Nishit appearing to be concerned said, "No, I think they appeared to be hurrying away from this place. This place surrounded by many trees, appears not safe."

Suddenly, they heard sounds like those of thunders, though the sky was clear.

Charudas expressing surprise, "What could be those thunder like sounds without any clouds on the sky, I wonder."

Another aged man said, "It sounded like the roar of a wild animal. Let's make it fast now."

The walk now transformed into run. The sound appeared to be unusual among the wild animals they came across in that forest until then. It was not certainly that of a milder class.

They hastened the walk further. They could not see anything through the jungle of short trees.

Suddenly, at a distance behind them they heard a bigger roar and a loud cry of a man in mortal fear.

Now they heard the footsteps of a person running behind them.

Veera looked back and saw at a distance a man running towards them. Farther behind him, a tiger held a man by his throat in its jaws and was trudging away into the woods. He was stunned. He had seen a tiger only in the circus before, while in the school. A tiger at close quarters was not expected by him, though he was in the midst of a forest. He was frightened beyond limits. Some others also saw that frightening sight. It was hard to believe, to look at a tiger, living and free, so close. They were stupefied with terror and stuck to the ground without movement.

One of the visitors, while running shouted, "It is a tiger dragging away a man into the trees."

With that all of them came to senses and to the real world and its strange happenings sometimes.

Chandra could not make a step further. She sank to the ground though conscious.

Veera pulled her up by the shoulders trying to drag her away, "Get up we have to run for our lives."

Sharad came forward to help him, by holding the other hand of the woman, but was checked by her husband.

Veera was almost carrying her away.

All others were walking fast away from the scene of the ghastly incident, looking back now and then with fear.

Nishit recovering somewhat, said "But nobody warned us about tigers in this place."

That incident rattled Charudas.

He uttered in low voice, "I never saw a tiger so close, that too dragging away a human being. That was most frightening."

"Yes, but I wonder why that person walked alone and was not with his group of visitor," said Nishit.

In the meantime, the person who was running towards them from behind joined them. They all forgot about that man, engrossed about their own safety.

He was trying to speak but could not. He was wide eyed and in a stupor. His dress was drenched in perspiration.

Charudas gave him water from his bottle. He helped him take it, as the later was not able to hold the bottle.

He recognized that man and asked anxiously "Brahma, what happened? Where is your friend Nanda?"

Brahma was crying inconsolably. He was looking at Charudas, but appeared as if he had not recognized him. Though he was looking at him, his mind was elsewhere. He was completely engrossed with the tragic incident from which he was saved.

After some persuasion, he started speaking in intermittent expressions "Nanda was struck by the tiger while we were on our way to this place. It took him away into the trees."

He started weeping again. After some consolation by his companions, he became silent and thinking, thinking of the disaster.

He was lost in his thoughts, while looking down.

"Come on now, let's walk fast. There is a village nearby." Nishit said.

The surroundings became dimmer now. The sun went down behind the trees. The pace of walk increased again.

Veera looking at an elderly man who was next to him asked, "Does this wild animal menace persist even after reaching the higher regions?"

The old man replied, sympathetically patting him on the back, “No, no. This forest area ends here. After crossing the valley, we are free of these dangers. The tiger would not go beyond the valley.”

The stars began appearing on the blue sky one by one. At a distance, they saw the lights of the village dwellings in the dark, competing with the stars in the sky.

They all walked towards the village choultry. The piercing cries of sheep and goats returning to the village for the evening, were resounding the surroundings.

Men and women there wore hill tribe’s dresses. The village choultry made of clay and stones had a large hall in the middle, surrounded by verandahs on all the four sides. The front verandah was lit by kerosene lamps.

As the visitors approached the hall, the guard’s wife cleaned the hall and the rooms. They lit two more lamps.

Then they enquired what each visitor wanted to eat. They brought hot milk and rotis with vegetable curry.

After having dinner, the visitors assembled in the front verandah. Brahma was crying with the recollection of Nanda. After persuasion by his companions, he ate a few rotis reluctantly.

Charudas resting his back against the wall said, “We are all afraid of tigers so much. But you may wonder to know that there was a man who used to kill tigers—mind you not one but many—with his bare hands.”

“I certainly will not believe it. Because you are a storyteller, you may be narrating a story to us. It’s simply not possible for a human being to kill a tiger with bare hands.” Veera responded at once.

"What I told is true. It is not a fable—neither from a storybook nor written by me. He was a strong athletic man, who used to go into the forest, to the place where tigers roam about and challenge a tiger in its own abode. He used to hit it with his bare hands between eyes. The tiger receives the shock of its life and dies on the spot."

"How you came to know about that man?" Nishit asked him.

Charudas turning towards him answered, "There is a book written by an Indian saint of great repute. He lived most of his life in U.S.A., preaching spiritual values and practice. He wrote about this strong man in that book."

"What is the name of that book?" Veera asked.

"Its title is, 'Autobiography of a Yogi'. It is the biography of that saint himself."

"But tiger is a fearsome animal. Whosoever sees it would become awestruck and immobilized. Not only that, the muscles of a tiger, they say are like steel wires, as William Blake described in his poem." That was Nishit's doubt.

"I am not denying it. However, suppose a person is very strong and trained to fight. Let us say he is very bold too. He is active and as fast moving as a tiger. Then such a person can challenge, attack and kill a tiger. He killed a number of them."

Brahma was listening to their conversation attentively. His fear was gone. He regained confidence and came closer to them now.

Sharad smiling and tightening muscles of the mouth in comic seriousness said "With this revelation, I am confident enough to kill at least one tiger when I encounter him next time."

"For that you need to walk alone in the forest, for which I think you will not find time."

Nishit said, indirectly hinting the other's lack of courage.

Sharad made no comment on that.

Charudas addressing Brahma, "Brahma, I guess you missed Nanda very much."

Brahma in pitiably low voice "Yes sir, we both planned this trip and started from our place."

Charudas to make him talk asked, "Was he very intimate to you?"

"Yes, we lived in the same town since more than a decade. We used to help each other in times of necessity. We discussed and planned to go to the last camp and return with the treasure. Now I am alone. The charm of the trip is gone"

"We are here with you. Try to forget the loss. My sympathies are with you. There is a saying, '*the only way to circumvent the pathos of loss of a close kin is to cultivate the habit of loving everyone around you, expecting no reciprocation.*' " Charudas consoled him.

"Moreover it's the fate that decides. When both are in the same situation, you are saved. You must thank God for that. You are saved for some reason. I am not telling you to be selfish but that is the fact. You can help his family in times of necessity," Veera said.

"Anyway, we cannot calm a person deep in tragedy by the explanation of fate, karma and so on," Charudas said.

"When saints meditate in the forests, even wild animals moving around the place become docile."

"That is because those saints had an aura around them which influences the nature of persons living there."

"We have not come across any such saints in these parts."

Nishit said, "I think they stay away from human habitats so as not to be disturbed. Let us hope we see such saints on our further trekking."

"What happened to Ramsaran and friends? They are not seen now." Charudas realized suddenly about their absence.

"That is surprising me too. They were with us till yesterday. I don't know what happened to them."

"They are young boys. They must have joined some others. We may see them again later," Chandra said.

"My only worry is about their safety. They are young and naturally hasty," Charudas said.

"But they are from villages and lived near forest. Ramsaran himself told us that. So I think they can take care of themselves," said Veera.

"They might have had the scent of the naxalites, which could have prompted them to run away. Police officials may not venture into these forests, but it is not the case with the naxals," said Sharad.

Charudas asked Sharad, "Do you know how this naxalism came into existence?"

"I only knew that it was a mass movement started in a place called Naxalbari in Bengal."

"That is correct. It all started when tribal land was usurped by landlords at Naxalbari in 1967. The tribal people rose in revolt against the landlords and regained their land."

Another in the group of visitors said, "But I know many students too joined the movement."

Yes, the earliest form of the movement which was a precursor to naxalism was the Telangana struggle in the south India. It was based on the ideology of Mao Zedong. In sixties and seventies, it was popular and many students including some from the engineering and other professional colleges too joined the movement. But over the years, the naxal movement lost its vision and compromised on its principles. Of course it still draws men and women who believed in its ideology.

In response to this struggle, landlords started local armies to protect themselves."

"Poor villagers like Ramsaran suffered in the cross current of hatred between the cadres and the landlords," said Nishit.

"We don't know how many in need of the support were helped. But we know the suffering of the villagers at the hands of these two groups and another agency that is the police." Another in the group opined.

IV

As usual they started early in the morning after the ablutions and breakfast, whatever that could mean in those circumstances.

They followed the existing footpaths. For confirmation, they take the guidance of older fellow visitors. Sometimes, they come across villagers who would direct them to the correct path. If nobody was there to guide, they might go astray and return to the correct path after trial and error, later. However, such occasions were not many. Nearer the villages, the paths formed on the mountain were many because villagers would go on errands to different places.

Now the direction they took was westward. The surroundings became colder than before but not difficult. When the sunrays fell on the moist breeze, there was a diffusion of rain bow colors on the western sky; opposite to those small trees, the mountain top covered by the greenery and above that white clouds; still above the partially visible blue sky with yellow and orange colored clouds, gave diverse, strange and beautiful sights to the fortunate viewers.

The visitors were now trekking down into the valley like region. The awe-striking sights nature had bestowed on them made them spellbound. They could not even share their impressions with each other; each one was engrossed in his own thoughts and joy.

Varied types of birds hovered over the sky. Some were flying away to unknown destinations. Some villagers were going on their errands.

The path now became wider with rows of trees on either side. In response to the sounds of footsteps of the visitors, there were bristling sounds in the grass and shrubs underneath the trees—snakes and other creatures moving to safer places. After going further, they came across a stream of water on their way. The crystal-clear water was flowing fast from one group of hills to another, but the level was low, showing the small stones beneath. Fish swam away avoiding the feet of the visitors. A bit away from the path, baby turtles were making a beeline towards the water. The visitors walked through the water reaching the other side. The path now led them to a higher terrain, another mountain.

At a distance from the right side of the path, a stranger in his early thirties was walking briskly towards them. He now joined them, obviously to trek further on the mountain in their company. He was in a long white shirt and pyjamas, with village-made sandals on his feet. His face was radiant. He talked to them with a friendly smile.

Charudas addressed him, "Where from you have materialized my dear young friend? Are you not afraid to go alone in these places?"

He expressed his surprise. Others too wondered about his sudden arrival.

The stranger replied with a smile, "I am not new to these parts. I sometimes pray sitting on that large stone there."

He pointed to a large stone lying beside the path at some distance.

"My name is Sudhama. I came here a week back. This is my second trip to these parts." He continued.

"Did you reach the last camp?" enquired Charudas.

"No. three months back, I went up to the fourth camp."

Veera asked him, "What work you do?"

"My father has cultivable lands. So I help him in cultivation."

"Don't you have brothers, who could help your father during your absence?"

"I have a step brother. But he is not nice to my father."

"I wonder how at this young age you developed such interest in spiritual pursuits."

Chandra asked him, "What about your marriage? Are you not going to marry?"

"How about your mother?" asked Veera.

"She is no more. She died when I was two. My father married again."

"Then you must have suffered persecution by your step mother." Chandra guessed.

Sudhama lowered his eyes. He did not reply.

"I know, it is a difficult situation in life. I too suffered for the same reason. And I was married off to a widower. Anyway I don't recollect those bad days. I am sorry to have brought back your unpleasant memories."

"Now I understand, that must be the reason for your detachment towards your family at early age," Veera said.

Charudas intervened, "That need not be the only reason. By nature some persons are philosophical. When they experience some painful incidents, those feelings are aroused and possibly increased. For others, those circumstances may drive them into the company of bad elements and they too become evil."

Sudhama did not speak.

Veera asked Sudhama, "What treasures are there at the top? I mean in what shape?"

His wife asked anxiously, "Do you think anything is left there yet, because so many people go there every day?"

Sudhama sympathetically "From what I know, those treasures never exhaust, in whatever shape they are."

"You mean to say, they won't be depleted, though so many people snatch away so much since many years," said Veera.

"Yes, they are unlimited and incidentally the number reaching there are not so many as you imagine."

Charudas with a smile "It's strange though. It appears to be true and logical, because the number of visitors is not dwindling even after so many days, may be even decades."

Nishit while increasing his pace said, "If we walk faster, we may reach the third camp by evening."

Sudhama correcting him "We already crossed that. You missed the third camp, as you traveled by a different route. You have to look for the fourth camp now."

Chandra still in fear of tigers, "Are you sure there won't be any tigers on our way here after?"

Sudhama with a reassuring smile answered "Certainly not. Dangers occur to much extent depending on our mental state."

Charudas asked, "What do you mean by that?"

"It's not my opinion. In fact, this is what our wise men say. When you are afraid, even a piece of rope appears as a snake. '*Rajju sarpa bhranthi*'."

Charudas slightly hurt "You mean that danger is only a mental status?"

The visitors there were all ears to the discussion.

Sudhama with a benign smile "Based on the mental status, the accident occurs. '*Yadbhavam thad bhavathi*'."

Veera without any expression on his face "We saw a friend of Brahma, accompanying him on this journey fell victim to the tiger, though he himself was not hurt."

"It happened just a day before, we cannot forget that," said Chandra.

Brahma was listening without a comment. His face became ashen, with the rekindled memory.

Sharad sarcastically "By his mental status, Brahma was saved from the attack of tiger."

Sudhama did not say anything.

All of them were still walking fast. They recollected the tragic incident of the previous day. So, they all wanted to reach the safe haven of next camp, or village.

A saintly man sat on a large rock in meditation by the side of the path.

Now it started to rain; it was like a shower.

Charudas said, "We are never sure of rain or sun in these mountains."

He was tired and impatient.

The rain had become intense now. They ran towards the trees besides the pathway.

Chandra shouted in surprise, "Look there on that rock; that saint praying there. He is not getting wet in the rain."

It was true that rain left the saint without drenching. The place around him too was dry. He was not disturbed from his meditation.

Charudas appreciating the phenomenon "It's great. I never saw such a miracle. He must be a great saint."

Sudhama looked at that saint without any comment.

"We may come across many more such feats in the days to come, as these parts appear to be favorite spots for meditation." Nishit said.

The rain subsided now. That saint did not move. He sat cross-legged, without any disturbance.

Brushing off the droplets on the head and dresses, the pilgrims resumed their ordeal once more. The ground was not marshy. It was not a bad exercise.

They did not come across another village on the way for some time. It was past midday. As they were preoccupied with walking and talking, they did not think of food. But the housewife's instinct in Chandra brought to their notice the necessity of eating.

They all assembled under a tree nearby and opened their packets of rotis and began eating.

Veera and Chandra shared some rotis with Sudhama, who did not refuse it.

While they were eating, two deer came near them, unusual though for wild animals anywhere else.

Sudhama fed them a few pieces of roti from his palm, which they ate without any fear or hesitation.

The visitors looked around for water. But they could not locate any lake or stream.

One of the deer, in the meantime, began pulling away the bark on the trunk of a nearby tree. Water flowed out of the trunk in a small trickle. Both the deer sipped the water.

"These deer are guides to us now. So we can safely follow their example," Sudhama said.

They quenched their thirst as the deer did.

Now the trek has become easy and less taxing.

Veera said looking around, "In this area trees are very few. We see some goats too."

"Yes. It appears, we are close to some village," Nishit concurred.

"So our journey stops for the time being, once again." Chandra was elated.

"We are nearing a place for the night's stay," said Sudhama.

After walking further, they found some villagers. But they didn't look like village folk. They appeared to be educated and were well dressed. They cultivated their lands for food grains.

They saw rows of houses after coming near the village. The place appeared well planned. Though there were not many houses, the streets were neatly laid.

There was a village choultry in the center.

The choultry was well lit. The villagers were busy in singing prayers. The visitors too joined them. Sudhama left them and was gone.

The visitors had to make their own arrangement for food and milk. They were supplied the required materials for cooking. They did not see any shops in the village.

* * *

By sunrise, the pilgrims were getting ready. They got the breakfast ready and packed.

The journey continued once more, on to the higher regions of the Green Mountain.

Early morning sun was warm. Sudhama, met them on the way.

Nishit sarcastically asked him, "You disappeared somewhere in the night?"

Sudhama taking it easy, "I require some solitude now and then. Probably everybody needs it."

Nishit lost in thoughts "But it does not suit me to be alone. Memories haunt me."

Sudhama looking around to make sure that they were not in hearing range, "It seems you are bogged down with worries. You are angry and impatient with the world."

Nishit did not reply.

Sudhama looking at him in sympathy "I believe I may be of some help. You may lessen your burden by sharing your worries with me."

Nishit did not speak out. They walked together a few more steps. Sudhama heard him now weeping.

Though he was younger to Nishit in age, Sudhama came near him and patted him on the back tenderly, to console him.

Nishit did not object.

Sudhama then said to him "Tell me, what is that which is troubling you so much at this young age? You should have been bubbling with joy, at this phase of your life."

Nishit looked at him. The latter appeared peaceful with a radiant face. He felt confident to share his worry with the other.

Addressing Sudhama he said, "What you said is true. I may lessen worries to some extent by talking to you. Of course, it's not a matter worth telling others."

He began his life story "I am the only child to my parents. Ours is a well to do family. My father worked as a senior officer in government service. I studied in a boarding school. I completed my studies in a short time, as I was a good student. I did my post graduation in economics. After getting through the central services examinations, I joined the government service as a Group I officer.

My parents used to entertain progressive views in life. Regarding my marriage, they wanted to go for a girl from a family of lower status, which was not a normal practice. Of course, there was a reason for that. When a cousin of my father was married into a family of higher status, they had to face some unpleasant situations."

He stopped his story for a drink of cold water.

As it was midday, the pilgrims felt hungry. But whatever they brought had been consumed in breakfast session. Those who were going ahead of Sudhama and Nishit slowed down and looked back.

Chandra addressing Sudhama said "Is it true that those who meditate are above thirst and hunger?"

"I heard so. But in my case, I am not bestowed with such a boon. I understood your comment. I think we have to depend on the trees here. They would not let us down. There will be many fruit bearing trees if we go ahead further. There is no necessity for us to suffer from hunger and thirst. For drinking water, we may come across some lake or spring. Otherwise, we have the example set by the deer." Sudhama replied with a smile.

Chandra was happy for another reason.

"That's good. Women should be spared from the tedium of cooking at least during tours."

"It does not matter. Something or other to fill the stomach is okay" Veera was reconciled.

"That's a best thing—to eat fruits for filling the stomach. Only we have to get accustomed to it," said Brahma.

"That's right. When there is no other way, it's necessary to get accustomed to new methods," Sudhama opined.

They resumed the trek. Sudhama and Nishit slowed their pace, to fall behind.

Sudhama continued "Nishit, what happened next?"

Nishit looking at the distant hilltop, "They have fixed my marriage with Tara, a girl from a family of lower status. They are not rich. My in laws performed the marriage in low key. It was talk of the town for some time. We had good time for some days. Once the preliminary attractions had worn out, it had become difficult for Tara to adjust in our family. The habits and style of living were different at my home. My family members tried to accommodate her well into our family. As Tara was indifferent, it was not easy for her to mingle and assimilate into our household affairs.

Luckily for us, my transfer to a different place was proved to be a blessing in disguise.

Even that did not last long. One day a cousin of Tara came to our house. He was transferred in his job to the place where we lived.

That day when I returned home from office, Tara and her cousin were in the drawing room.

Tara introduced Rana to me. He was her paternal aunt's son. He was working as a sales man in some company.

Later on, he used to come to our house frequently. He used to frequent even when I was not home. She moved freely with him. It did not take much time for me to know her estimate of myself.

One evening I returned home by walk, as my office jeep broke down. By the time I reached home, Tara and Rana were in conversation, while sipping coffee. They did not notice me.

Tara said, "Do you know why these people of high status married their son to me? Even my father had a doubt about that. Now that proved to be correct. I suspect he has some deficiency."

Rana said smiling "Such things won't remain under wraps for long."

I was surprised and disgusted. Surprised because how she could talk such things with an outsider, I mean a third person and a man that too, though there was no truth in that. She was misrepresenting. It was disgusting to know, how low she stooped down to get intimate with that man. I felt bad to know that my in laws also were so mean. They gave that much value to our progressive views. While leading a happy life with me, I was amazed how she could spread such canards without an iota of truth. These things, as you know, are of such a sensitive nature, I could not discuss with anybody. Any person who comes to know of such things would be tempted to believe the negative aspect only. It is easy and fanciful for anybody to talk ill of others. It is the tendency of common people.

On thinking over the matter, I concluded that she behaved like this out of injured inferiority complex. Out of such inferiority complex arises superiority complex.

But I don't think any sane person would ruin her own life in such a way. She was misguided by Rana to resort to that kind of belief.

Another day I had to go on work to a place away from home. As I would not return home that night, I asked my friend's mother to keep company with Tara. She agreed to do so. After my return from camp, I came to know that Tara did not call her. When I enquired discretely, I found that Rana kept her company that night.

I warned Tara not to be so intimate with Rana. I also made it clear that people may misunderstand that closeness. I was amused hearing her reply. She said that they were like that since childhood and she would not care about other's opinions about that. I felt hurt.

After a few days, I learnt that people of the town began talking ill about Tara and Rana. My office staff also started commenting indirectly about my imaginary shortcomings.

Sometime later, I had to go on camp once more. Before that, I called my parents to come over to my place so that I could lessen my suffering. Moreover, that would give them an opportunity to know about my present life. Of course, I told them that Tara needed their company during my absence.

When I returned from camp, Tara was not home. My parents told me that she went out with Rana the previous evening. She did not return home even on the next day. My parents were shocked. Though I did not explain in detail, they could guess the condition in which I lived. I later made a call to my in laws. My wife did not go there. They blamed me for this situation.

Some days later, I got a notice from my wife's lawyers for divorce. She cited my impotence as reason for divorce petition. My father talked to my in laws. He did not get proper response from them. I accepted the divorce, to get rid of such an unwanted relationship. However, I cited her infidelity as the reason for acceptance of the divorce plea. Later I applied for long leave in my office. Divorce was granted to us in due course.

I did not return to my job after the leave. I am going around to different places to regain my peace of mind.

Nishit finished his life's story. He was walking with downcast eyes.

Sudhama said "Your life story is a strange one. The efficacy of the remedy for this depends on the individual's capacity to absorb the shock and on his resilience. Some weak hearted may resort to annihilating himself. I appreciate you for your strength to withstand and search for new life. A person who can understand the purpose of life will only be able to do like that. Some people turned towards God and achieved the highest goal. One can help others in need and render service. If the desire for achievement in life is strong, you can start afresh a life with new goals."

Nishit intercepting him said, "I am not bothered now about the past life. I am philosophical by nature. So I am not enamored by achievements of life. I am worried only about my parents who must be worried about my life and welfare."

Sudhama with a beaming face, "Of course, it's your responsibility to keep them happy. Unfortunately, you could not put your life on proper track even though you wished it. You were not at fault that the marriage was on rocks. It is the fate, which decides, largely. Your efforts could not change your fate. Then it is obvious that you cannot change the fate of your parents for better. It was entangled with your fate since your birth.

But I am not advocating a defeatist attitude. You should not neglect them. Help them to settle in a peaceful routine of life. If they have any special interest like writing, music or other fine arts, it is easy to fix them in life. If you give them some support they can engage themselves in that activity. Then you can choose your future course of action and work for it."

Nishit was satisfied with the explanation given by Sudhama.

He said with a smile, "Yes, that's what I did exactly. They were interested in social service. I have made my parents as members of an organization rendering social service. They are now busy with that occupation. As to myself, I am trying to settle down in life."

Nishit continued after a short silence, "However, it is hard to control the mind. Whatever methods I had adopted, past memories continue to return to destroy peace of mind."

Sudhama smiled, "So, controlling the mind is the only solution. Meditation is the method to do that."

"After conversing with you, I now feel that what you said must be true."

"Near the fourth camp, you may get better conditions to do that."

"Certainly, but you please guide me in that."

Sudhama nodded his head in acceptance.

Nishit with hesitation said, "I am surprised at your depth of knowledge. I don't believe that you are with our group in search of treasures."

He however was not sure of getting a reply to his query.

But Sudhama replied with a smile "What you said is correct. I am not in search of treasures. It took me a great deal of effort to convince my father that I would return home, after this trip. I have no difficulties at home. But from my childhood, I had a feeling that I should find out the purpose of this life. I now trust that I am on proper path."

He continued, "I believe everyone will act according to his instincts and attitudes of his previous birth, with modification to the extent of his effort made to improve in the earlier birth and the present one.

"For some, the effort they make is due to the difficulties they face and the determination they have to improve the status of their life. Some others may act according to the merits or demerits of previous birth only."

Nishit interrupted, "You are not clear. I am confident though, as we are on the same journey, I could get clarifications in future."

V

Vacra gave a punch on the back of Manda. He did not like his follower to walk before him, though by mistake. They had to learn the lesson the hard way.

Manda fell forward hitting the ground. He got up with a bleeding nose, while passing a side-glance at his boss, Vacra. It was a pitiable sight, but not to Vacra, the noted burglar in half the territory of Bihar. Manda was short and slow in action.

Vacra began laughing at his plight. Others around him followed suite.

Saral came to his rescue and helped him to his feet.

They were on their way to the Green Mountain from the western side. They knew that the route on this side was rough and unwelcome. But the number of people climbing up there was also less, making it a convenient route for those who did not want to be noticed for some reason.

Vacra was aged around forty years, athletic looking and attractive. He was awe-inspiring to his companions. He was a sharpshooter and could use many sorts of guns with ease. He got good grooming in his profession at his early childhood itself as the circumstances forced him so.

They were in pants and shirts and appeared to have learnt sophistication recently. Each one of them was carrying a couple of thick bags bulging at the seams with personal requirements for a long journey.

Vacra asked one of his companions "Shyama, what did the man in ochre robes tell you in the village?"

Shyama in all humility replied "Boss, he talked of the abundant treasures at the top of the Green Mountain. He commented that we were wasting our time in the towns and villages nearer home."

Vacra with a loud guffaw said, "I wonder how you came across that man."

Another in the group Grahi explained, "Boss, on that day myself and Shyama were returning after finishing our work at one of the rooms of the ashram."

Vacra interrupted with a beaming face "Of course it was a job well done. They were very rich."

Grahi continued, "Boss, when we were near ashram gate and on our way out, an inmate in ochre robes, called us back. But we did not go."

Shyama said with a smile, "We are not fools to go back."

"Yes, we know what to do. We hurled a stone at him. But he did not run away. He walked towards us with bare hands. So when he reached us, we did not hurt him. He explained about the Green Mountain and the treasures on top of it." Grahi said.

"That's great. After returning from this trip, we will reward him," Vacra said.

"Yes boss, he will be glad. We gave gifts to police many times," said Shyama.

By noon, they reached a clear place. They made a beeline to a big banyan tree. After clearing the area of dry leaves and twigs, the group settled under the tree. One of them opened the food sack full of packets and distributed them to each, starting with the boss.

After resting for some time, the group again started on their journey for treasure trove at the top of the mountain.

Now the path became narrow. They had to make way by breaking and cutting away branches coming in the way. It's not every day that people pass by that route.

One amongst the group, Manda suddenly felt lifted up high into the thick of tree branches. He could not breathe freely. Something was crushing his chest. He could neither see the object of trouble nor utter a sound.

Shyama who was behind him until then was aghast with terror. He saw a big snake curling up around Manda and lifting him up towards the tree branches on one of which it lay securely coiled around.

He shouted in fear, "Boss, a large snake is carrying away Manda."

Vacra and others who were a few feet ahead looked back to find Manda dangling in the air in the clutches of a big python. The boss did not lose nerve or time. After all, he was the leader of the group. He at once unfastened the pistol from his belt and aiming at the body of the python shot it, taking care not to hurt his companion in the act. The python in a sudden motion eased its hold on Manda. He was dropped to the ground. A few drops of blood fell on him from the body of the big snake. It remained there without any further motion. The pistol shot was neither grievous nor lethal to it. Obviously, it was a sudden pinprick sufficient enough for Manda to be dropped down.

The group of adventurers dashed forward away from the scene of the incident.

Shyama rolling his eye balls up in fear said, "The snake's body is as stout as the chest of Manda."

Manda still gasping for breath said, "It almost crushed me in its hold. I could not breathe freely."

"It's not as stout as his chest. It's about the size of thigh." Another man said.

Vacra without any visible emotion uttered, "It would have gulped away this fellow after a few minutes, had I not shot it at once. Of course it would not die. The pain—sudden pain—made it loosen its hold on this fellow."

Now, they all laughed away happily. They became tough and cruel in the course of their exploits in antagonistic situations.

It was becoming dark. They had to make a halt for the night. The terrain was new. It was not known, how safe it could be to sleep in the open, without any shelter and protection. They discussed about the plan for night halt.

"Boss, I know on the eastern side of the mountain, the pilgrims get accommodation and food on the way, of course on payment only," Saral said.

Vacra scornfully "So, what do you suggest?"

Manda with fear filled voice "If possible, boss, we could go over there. We would be safe in the night."

Vacra began laughing "Safety for us? Others should run for safety from us."

Shyama hesitantly "Boss, but the animals and snakes of the forest are dangerous and their attacks unpredictable."

Vacra appeared thoughtful for some time.

"But now what could we do? We should have planned that way in the beginning. By night, we must reach nearby camp. For this night, we must stay in some clear place. Tomorrow onwards, we must plan as I said," He said.

Others did not utter a word. After all, he was the boss. There would not be any arguments comments or amendments.

After walking for some time, they found a place, which was higher than the surrounding ground. A rocky place it was. It was like a platform. There were no trees nearby. They made it the place to stay for the night.

They lit fire on all the four sides of the place where they were to sleep.

It was decided that the fire must burn the whole night. A night vigil was to be observed. Every four hours the guard would be changed. The round the night plan was in place. They ate sitting around the campfire. Sufficient quantity of firewood was collected. One of them caught a stray and unlucky rabbit, which became food for them instantly.

With the newfound food source, they made it a point to hunt for a few animals every day to provide a more nourishing side dish. Of course, it was necessary for them for their tough work ahead, the trekking of the mountain. The ultimate reward was worthwhile. Once they laid their hands on the treasures, it would take care of their lives and might be their children's too. There was no necessity to work anymore. Here the risks attached were not as bad as that of the difficult and uncertain work such as theirs. They discussed and discussed until they became tired and sleepy.

The guards during the night vigil saw burning eyes at a distance. But no animal came near the camp fire. They could also catch a few animals during the early dawn for consumption later.

Thus, they had special items of animal meat for breakfast. Vacra said that energizing food was a necessity for the hard work they had ahead of them. Their normal work did not entail such hardship as this. Of course it involved risk—risk of injuries to the body—risk to life too sometimes—of course rarely so.

As they wanted to trek up the mountain from the eastern side, they changed the direction of movement now, to the right side that means to the southern side.

Vacra forced his companions to walk fast, lest others might go to the crest of the mountain earlier to them. He occasionally cautioned them against the chance of losing the treasures to the early birds—in entirety or a portion. He was loath to share any amount with others.

After trekking for a few hours, they had a tingling feeling in the mouth—for tea. They were accustomed to that. After all they were townspeople.

Vacra could not bear it any longer.

"My friends, we must have tea now. Anybody has ideas to get a cup of tea for each one of us?" He asked.

His companions began discussing amongst themselves. Finally they resolved that one of them must go for scouting and after locating the tea-shop, get a pot-full of it either for payment or otherwise.

Vacra decided that as they were going towards southern side, the person in search of tea-shop should go towards the left side—that was eastern side of the mountain. Going by northern route was tough with more difficult terrain and longer way. They knew that tea-shops abound on the path on eastern side of the mountain.

Then the question arose who should go on that job. Manda was a dull man, so was not capable of doing anything alone. Shyama was all right, but he was hot tempered. Here tact and resourcefulness were necessary. After weighing all the factors, they zeroed in on Saral.

Saral was advised to walk clear of trees to avoid any attacks by animals. He was asked to take a path free of possible dangers and at the same time not very close to the human habitats, where law-enforcing agencies may be lurking and prowling. They were as dangerous as wild animals.

Saral went ahead eastward, of course sufficiently armed. He looked for symbols of human presence, like broken twigs, paths made by regular treading and so on. After walking further, he could see burnt out cigarettes and empty packets, etc. and in due course of time he heard human voices. He finally reached the place he was looking for—a tea-shop.

The tea-shop he reached was not crowded. He paid for the pot-full of tea. And without many words he retraced his steps back towards the place, where he started from, so that he could meet his companions on the way. While in the shop, he heard those present there mentioning that it was close to camp two.

When the tea was brought, there was jubilation in the camp. They made a fire, which was easy with the plenty of broken and dry twigs found around the place. The teapot was heated up. They felt the hot tea tasted well and better than any tea available elsewhere, as the item was a rare commodity in the midst of that jungle.

Saral made it known to all that they were close to camp two, which means four more camps to reach the top, the haven of treasures.

The trek up the hill was resumed. The enthusiasm in pursuit of treasures was doubled after knowing that they had passed two camps already. Vacra described that as good progress. One third of the hard task was finished by the end of the third day. At that rate by next week, they should be laying their hands on the treasures. At this point Vacra's imagination took wings—the wings were losing thrust due to the knowledge that he was coming across resistance or obstruction—obstruction in the shape of other hands risen to pick from those treasures. He was not a person who would lose race to others. He never allowed others to come close to his earnings or those he sighted.

Vacra thought that he must lessen the competition for the riches at the top. But how?

His resourceful and demonic mind began planning. At the mildest, he could scare the visitors by different means. He could misguide them too. After that—probably at the higher camps—nearer the treasures—he must eliminate competition—at any cost. Now he looked at his men, eight altogether, including himself. Was it a big number to share with? A smile spread across his face thinking about that. He thought he could only disclose his first stage of plans—namely to scare away other groups from different places and sides of the mountain—the Green Mountain.

They walked and walked until they were tired. The sun now reached zenith. At one place, they found water in the depression of a big rock, a single rock, jet black and smooth as the skin of a maiden. In the center of that rock, four feet deep hollow formation was there. It was a natural formation full of clean water. They drank the clean water and made a store of it in the sacks they brought.

Vacra asked his companions to stop for lunch. A few rotis remaining in the bag were not sufficient. Manda was the cook for the group. They had a few rabbits and birds caught on the way. Other members of the group helped him in cooking. After an hour, they had a satisfying lunch.

Vacra lied down on a bed sheet spread on the ground under a large tree, after the heavy lunch. Some of his companions followed suit.

Suddenly those who were awake heard some voices at a distance. Shyama looked at that side keenly and found them to be a police party in uniforms and with guns. He discreetly woke up Vacra and others, who were sleeping. They all then hid behind a thick screen of tall grass in between the trees. The police party moved away towards east.

After making sure, the police were far away, the group of Vacra started on their journey.

Shyama had a doubt now.

"Boss, I have a doubt why the police party is not after the treasures?" He asked Vacra.

Vacra said without taking any time to think, "They are a set of lazy people. They will convince themselves that this is all a futile exercise. They are clever enough however and if they find anybody with treasure, they would quote some rule and confiscate it for government. Some portion of it may reach government if any witness is there. Otherwise even that won't be spared."

"That's right. In that case there is no necessity for them to tire themselves out for it," Shyama said.

The trek was going on. It had to continue. It required a big hope, constant effort and tenacity. No piece meal returns like the works they undertake; this required a few days hard work without any doubts. It's like a penance.

Some in the group were married. Vacra thought of his only child, a boy, a few times. But his wife knew that her husband was to be left to himself for a few days, every now and then. He did not tell her about this adventure. It was prompted by the information provided by Shyama and Manda. The hint given by the inmate of the ashram made him plan this trip. It was a change from the routine. But as agreed by all of them, it was a journey worth undertaking for a fulfilling life's desire.

Vacra while smoking his country cigar said, "This evening we must reach some nearby village or whatever they call it a 'camp'. It would be safe for the night and also takes care of the night's meal and breakfast in the morning."

They all agreed. It would be less work for them too. Otherwise, they had to prepare for night vigil and cook food for all.

"Boss, now it's a must for us to reach some village by evening, because we don't have any food left," Saral said.

As the sun was lowering itself over the horizon, this group of aspirants began diverting walk towards the east, to reach some village.

Before it was dark, they reached a village on the eastern side. They met the village head and sought shelter and food. The dialogue went on as follows.

Village head, "Who are you people?"

Vacra "We are from town of Gangapatna and we want some place to sleep tonight."

"But you don't look like those from that place. We do not allow strange people here. There were thefts and other problems before. It's better to be curt now, than suffering later."

Vacra felt insulted and became angry.

"You villagers are very suspicious. But you can do nothing, when something adverse happens to you." He blurted out.

Village head's son who heard this dialogue got offended.

He said angrily, "You have come here for seeking a favor and you dare to insult us. You can go away now."

Vacra's followers intervened and begged the senior for accommodation for night's stay.

Vacra walked away from the scene. After some time the village head reluctantly asked them to stay in the hutment attached to the cattle sheds. The son of the village head went away laughing loudly at the outcome.

The travelers who were eight in number including their boss then walked towards the cattle sheds, as there was no other go.

Vacra asked Saral to check whether any other accommodation could be secured in the village for rent. Saral left at once.

The hutment attached to the sheds was neatly kept. Bamboo cots with jute ropes were there for some. Two hurricane lanterns threw dim light around. Some servant boys were already sleeping there. Obviously, the huts were meant for servant boys.

"Boss, why some cots are not occupied still?" One of the followers of Vacra asked him.

"They might have gone for the mates."

"Where do they get mates?" He asked feigning innocence.

"Where else, you fool; at close quarters—the landlord's women." Vacra laughed loudly.

He was angry with the landlord for the accommodation given to them.

Vacra lowered himself on one of the vacant cots. He was smiling within himself at the repetition of fate. He remembered his childhood days. He lived those times in similar conditions. But things were different now. He owned a nice building in the town all by himself.

His chain of thoughts was disturbed.

Saral returned from the job he was assigned.

“What happened? Any better accommodation is there?” Vacra asked.

“No boss, I am afraid we have to spend the night here only.” Saral said solemnly.

Contrary to the expectation of his companions, Vacra said, “Be it so. We will sleep here.”

They talked about that unpleasant decision of the boss with each other in low voices and concluded that there must be some reason for the decision of the boss.

Vacra then sent another companion to bring something to eat.

After finishing eating, they drank the water kept there for the servant boys. They slept well in spite of the bad conditions there, as they were very tired after the continuous trek.

Early in the morning, Vacra woke up one of his companions who slept close to him and asked him to get everybody ready for the journey again.

Each one of them secured whatever he thought would be useful on the way, from amongst the things available there in the large hut. There were bed sheets, some large sticks, farm implements and so on.

VI

A group of monks had a dip in the river Narmada. They wrapped their bodies in dry clothes, a dhoti and an upper cloth. The wet garments, they laid on the rocks on either side of the path to the hills. By the time the sun rises up in the sky, the clothes would get dried up by the currents of heavy winds blowing from the forests surrounding the hills. The group of mendicants was on their way to the Green Mountain.

The small band of ascetics was led by swami Anandagiri, who had an ashram in Brindavan. As the sun rose up, the swami called his disciples to collect their clothes spread on the large rocks for drying up and resume their journey. The swami was aged forty and his disciples were in the age group of twenty plus to thirty.

As the parents in any household have their preferred child, the swami had a soft corner for his disciple Sudhanva, who used to attend to his guru more often and more attentively.

Sudhanva was an orphan. His parents died when he was of a tender age of two. One of his uncles was entrusted with the upbringing of the child. The boy grew up to the age of eight with him. His uncle did not want his nephew to suffer any further at the hands of his merciless wife and hence took the boy to the ashram of swami Anandagiri. Swami Anandagiri agreed to take care of the boy in his ashram. As the boy expressed his liking for the life of a mendicant, he took him later as one of his disciples.

Sudhanva approached his guru and asked him respectfully, "Swami, may I know the purpose of our journey to the mountains?"

Even though they started five days back from their ashram, the disciples did not know why they were heading towards the mountains situated in the deep north. In a way, they liked the journey to get away from the routine. They were not new either, to the pilgrimages as the inmates were not supposed to stay at one place getting used to the comforts of mundane life. But lack of proper food on the days of journey was foremost of the difficulties. Each one of the disciples had his own story to tell as to why he joined the band of monks. For some it was a heart-felt necessity. One of them did not want to pursue the routine studies of school, college and so on. He was interested in studying the ancient culture and knowledge. In the case of some other, Maruthi, his father wanted to make his son a religious head.

Swami looked around at the faces of his disciples who were thinking and waiting for his answer.

He said with a smile, "We are heading towards the Green Mountain, on top of which we could find a wish tree. It is the path way to the ultimate, the pinnacle of joy, which resides on top of it. Each one of you could get his wish fulfilled, be it worldly desire or spiritual accomplishment. But it depends on individual effort, to reach the top."

The guru wanted to help his disciples to achieve their aspirations—each on his own, as he himself decided to. He knew he could take care of them during that arduous journey.

Another of the group who was agitated to know about the task ahead asked the guru in anxiety, "Sir, if one of us is not able to bear the strain or could not make it like others, what will happen to him?"

The guru replied in comforting words, "You need not worry about that. If somebody could not make it he would stay at ashrams on the way safely. He has two options, either to stay in that ashram or return to Brindavan later."

Now on the way they came face to face to a big boulder, obstructing the way. They had to pass through a narrow passage encircling the large rock to continue with the journey.

They just passed the obstructing boulder, and reached the path on the other side. When they made a few steps further, they heard a small growl and were stunned to see a cheetah opposite them. But the swami did not utter a word or moved from where he stood. He became stone like, looking ahead at the beast. The disciples followed suite. They had abundant faith in him.

The panther after a few moments went way.

Sudhanva asked the guru, "Sir, how long it will take to reach the top?"

The guru smiled enigmatically and replied, "It all depends on how energetic we are and the enthusiasm we evince. Of course, one must be blessed to gain the ultimate joy. So pray to the lord for your success, each one of you."

The mountain track became steep after the bend at the big obstructing boulder. The young ascetics however did not find it difficult to climb.

By midday, they made good progress and rested under a large tree. Before starting on the journey, each one of the five disciples was given a good hoard of fruits and rotis, which they carried in a sack on their back.

Now they opened their sacks of food and began eating. Their guru too gulped a few bananas. The ground was covered with round smooth rocks. So for the bare footed young men it was not hurting to walk. The guru asked his disciples to walk faster, so that they could reach some human habitat by evening. He said it might not be safe to linger in the forest–like mountain terrain much longer.

One of the disciples Maruthi asked his guru, “But sir, you said ascetics need not fear anybody or anything. Do you consider it unsafe even for us?”

His guru replied with a smile, “My dear young one, as far as possible we will take care to protect ourselves. We will follow the normal dharma of humans. Only when it is willed by God, we will take his help.”

When they reached a village, they met a cowherd boy whom they asked about the location of the village temple. He gave sufficient guidance to reach the temple. They crossed the arch at the entrance of the village and came to a large well. The disciples went near it. The village women who were drawing water gave way to the mendicants after paying obeisance to them. The visitors filled water in the pitchers they carried and then proceeded to the temple.

When they reached the temple, already some villagers were waiting for them. Obviously, the message reached them even before the visitor's arrival there. The villagers paid respects to the ascetics as per the custom. Then they asked them whether they require anything for the night's stay. The mendicants did not desire anything. However, after a few moments servants of the village head brought a few pots of milk and some fruits. The guru asked the priest of the temple to offer them to the deity, Lord Siva. After the usual prayers, a small part of it was taken by visitors.

At the instance of the guru, the villagers sat there on the mats spread over the ground. The guru sat facing them, on one side of the elevated platform surrounding the temple. The disciples sat at a respectable distance from their guru.

The head of the village asked the guru, "Swami, where are you going with your disciples?"

The guru replied, "We are coming from our ashram in Brindavan. These are my disciples, Sudhanva, Maruthi, Nandabala, Omkara and Viswam. I am called Anandagiri. We are on our way to the top of Green Mountain. Tomorrow morning we start on our further journey."

The farmer whose cowherd boy was instrumental in informing about the arrival of the group to the village then asked the swami, "Swami, we know that the Green Mountain has treasures on its top. But how you as ascetics are interested in the treasures? We are at a loss about this?"

The swami with a broad smile across his face replied, "I don't know about the treasures as I was never interested in them. But we are going there in search of more valuable thing than that."

The head of the village asked the swami in surprise, "But swami, is there anything greater than treasures?"

The swami, "You tell me, have you seen anybody who was not interested in more money though he already is a rich man. What does that mean?"

All those who assembled there were silent.

The swami continued, "It shows that no amount of money gives the satisfaction, the people seek for. Something is there which is greater than material pleasures. We are after that."

The villagers assembled there did not understand the meaning of that. But they were confident that the swami must be capable of bestowing some benefits like curing of diseases and so on. Anyway by asking for some kind act, they were not going to lose anything, but if he was powerful they would be benefited. That was the simple villagers' logic.

So, one of them hopefully asked the ascetic, "Swami, I don't have any children. Please help me by suggesting some ritual for fulfilling our desire. My wife is bed ridden with that worry only."

The swami looking at that man said, "I understand your pain. There must be some reason, why you are not begetting children like others. It depends on many factors."

He closed his eyes and stopped speaking for a few moments.

He resumed, "I assure you, if you live loving other's children like yours, one day you will certainly be blessed with a child. This is God's law. If you have sufficient love in your heart even for others children, you will at once attract a boon for a child."

Another villager brought his sick child to the swami and asked for his grace to cure the child.

He said with tearful eyes, "Swami, this child of mine is sick since six months and no medicine could cure him from this malaise. Kindly help him to get rid of this misery."

The swami asked the villager to give his son a piece of the fruit previously offered to the Deity there, after praying to Him. The swami himself closed his eyes in prayer.

After a few moments the boy opened his eyes, got up to his feet and asked his father for some more fruits to eat, as he was feeling hungry. The villager and his son prostrated before the swami in respect and gratitude. The villagers present there too paid obeisance to the swami.

After arranging for the swami and his disciples night's stay, the villagers left them.

The mendicants then sat in meditation for a long time before they slept.

The guru and his followers resumed their journey next day. They continued to follow the clearer way up the mountain. It was no ready laid road. Their guru took care to see that his disciples were not put to pain by walking on difficult terrain or thorny bushes. They did not wear any footwear for protection.

After walking the whole day, they reached a place where there were caves, some deep and some others not so. The guru selected a cave not very deep, to avoid encountering any wild animal. He explained that in some caves they might find some spiritual-minded persons in meditation, even at that height. They should not disturb them.

In one corner, they saw some light throwing soft glow around. Just above that place, there was a hole in the top of the cave showing the starlit sky. Some kind of stones at that spot absorb the sunlight during the day and give the glow during the night, to provide light to the occupants.

It took time for the disciples to get sleep, as they travelled on empty stomach that day.

After the night's rest, they resumed the trek again next morning. On the way, they had bath in a small lake formation in the rocks. The guru picked some kind of berries found on bushes and ate them. His followers too ate them. They found the berries very tasty.

The group of mendicants from the north had the sun straight on their face, as they were to take a diversion towards the east as a large waterfall obstructed the way. After walking for some time, they began hearing human voices at a distance. Presently, they came face to face with a group of aspirants from the eastern side of the mountain.

One of them Saka made obeisance to the guru. Others followed suite. Now the merged bigger group of travellers continued their journey with vigor as the entourage gave them the encouragement.

Saka asked the guru why even people like him, who had forsaken all worldly temptations, could not withstand the lure of treasures. The group from east did not take kindly to the intrusion of aspirants from north.

The guru gave the same reply as he did to the villagers a few days back. But Saka was not satisfied with that reply.

He commented to his companion, "All these ascetics are like this. It is hard to suppress the worldly desires, you know."

His companion replied, "That's right. But they have an advantage over us. They know some tricks by which they can reach the top faster than us."

So the first man asked the guru, "Swamy, why don't you share some tricks with us? I know you have knowledge of some."

He then prostrated at the feet of the guru.

The disciples of the guru were taken aback with this sudden development.

They tried to explain that they had been traveling like all others and that in fact they had no food the previous day. At this, others in the group of Saka were infuriated.

They now suspected that those mendicants were not ready to divulge the secrets and trying to suppress the truth. Moreover the guru and his disciples did not appear to be weak of starvation as given to by them. Their faces were bright and they were energetic though thin.

Saka then menacingly moved close to the guru and said, "If you don't reveal any such tricks and help us in this difficult journey, you cannot advance any more in your trek."

Another of his group pushed the guru back. The disciples tried to stop him, but could not as others too joined the first and they were more determined and well built.

The guru nevertheless did not get angry. He kept his calm. When many others joined, he raised his hand in protest and the miracle happened.

The troublemakers could not move any more towards the guru.

The guru then signaled his disciples to follow and they walked away from the scene of trouble. After making some distance, the disciples looked back and found nobody following them.

One of the disciples Sudhanva commented when he noticed that the guru was not in hearing range, "Maruthi, it is confusing to watch how our guru applies different methods of escape in different situations."

"Regarding what methods you are talking?"

"When we were confronted by the cheetah we all stood still and escaped. Now when those miscreants tried to attack, guru just raised his hand and they could not move and we walked away. Don't you think it's odd?"

"We cannot fathom the wisdom of the guru."

The guru slowed down his pace and after a pause said, "I would now narrate a story so that we will not feel monotony of the journey."

His disciples in one voice exclaimed in joy, "Yes guruji, we are eager to hear the story."

The guru began "Long time back, that was even before Lord Sree Rama was born, one king by name Ambareesh was ruling with Ayodhya as capital city. He was a great devotee of Lord Vishnu. He had a daughter whose name was Sreemathi.

One day Narada, the celestial singer who was the son of Lord Brahma—born by his wish—came to the court of king Ambareesh, accompanied by his nephew Parvathamuni. The king welcomed and offered fruits and drinks to them. He then asked what he could do for them. At that time their glances fell on the beautiful maiden standing by the side of the king. They were struck by her grace. Narada asked the king who that enchanting lady was. He replied that she was his daughter. Both Narada and Parvathamuni wanted to marry her. But they wanted to tell this to the king in privacy.

So they met the king separately, each without the knowledge of the other and told him about their desire to marry his daughter. The king was taken aback at the odd desire of the saintly persons. But he was confident that God whom he believed would not desert him in his travails. So he said that he venerated both of them and he did not want to go against their wish. But he said that it was necessary to find out the opinion of his daughter in this matter. And he further made it clear that whomsoever she likes, he would not have any objection to give her in marriage. After listening to him they said they would meet the king next day and took leave of him.

There is a saying that a person in love would be devoid of shame or fear. The celestial singer Narada went straight to Lord Vishnu in Vishnuloka. Without feeling any embarrassment, he said that he loved the daughter of king Ambareesha and wanted to marry her. He also informed the Lord that Parvatha also desired her and he should be kept out of the selection. He prayed the Lord that when the girl looked at Parvatha, his face must look like that of a monkey.

A smile passed over the face of the Lord and he promised that as he was one of His closest followers, his rare wish was granted. And so, when the lady looks at Parvatha she would only see the face of a monkey, the Lord declared.

Narada went away happily feeling that he secured Sreemathi for himself from the clutches of Parvatha.

After some time, Parvathamuni too approached Lord Vishnu and prayed to him to grant him the boon of marrying the king's daughter. He confided to Him that Narada was coming in the way and that the Lord must see that the other would not succeed. He desired that when the lady looked at Narada his face must appear like that of a monkey so that she would not like him.

The Lord said that he was satisfied with his prayers and that he granted that boon.

Next day, the princess came forward to garland one of the suitors, in the august assembly of the king attended by many nobles, ministers and the people.

The king was not worried about the outcome as he was sure of God's help in solving this problem thrust on him.

When she first looked at Narada she was afraid to see a monkey face with human body. Then she transferred her looks to Parvathamuni and cried in fear to see another monkey face.

The king enquired about her fears. She then explained that it was not Narada or Parvatha before her but only monkey faced humans. She also told that beside those monkey faces she saw a handsome young man with beautiful features and princely grace. All the assembled people were surprised to hear those words.

Narada then asked her to describe about that handsome person. She said that the prince was holding a big bow and arrows in his hands. He wore a garland of flowers around his neck.

The wise men assembled there declared that it could not be other than Lord Vishnu in that guise.

Narada then blamed the king for the outcome. But the king said he and his daughter did not know anything about what had happened.

The princess then with the blessings of her father and the wise men adorned the handsome young man standing in between the original suitors, with the garland. At once both the girl and the young man disappeared. The people assembled there were aghast with the sudden development.

Both Narada and Parvathamuni hanged their faces in shame.

They took leave of the king and went straight to the Vishnuloka. They could not find the princess there as expected by them. The Lord welcomed them. But Narada blamed Him for not keeping his word. Lord then narrated the incident of how after the departure of Narada, Parvthamuni came to Him and about his wish and so on.

When asked about the handsome person whom the princess married, Vishnu expressed his ignorance about that.

Narada at this became angry and he straight went to king Ambareesha. He declared that the king was at fault for what had happened and he would suffer the consequences. He cursed that the latter would lose all his knowledge and become an ignorant man.

Lord Vishnu knowing about the misfortune occurring to Ambareesha sent his powerful celestial disc to protect him. Narada could not withstand the power of the wheel coming after him to punish. He went to the Lord seeking protection.

Lord Vishnu said Ambareesha was also a devotee to him like Narada and hence he had to protect him. Then he withdrew his disc.

Narada could not control his anger though a saintly person himself and he said that the Lord would also suffer like him. He would take birth in the family of king Ambareesha and marry Sreemathi, with the same form as that young handsome person who took her away from him. But he would lose her to an enemy to regain later, but again to lose her forever.

So as cursed by the celestial singer the Lord took the form of Sree Rama and suffered all the troubles as uttered by Narada."

The guru completed the story.

He went to a water source trickling down from the upper hills, to quench his thirst. His disciples followed him.

Maruthi now asked the guru, "But why should the Lord obey the utterance of his devotee?"

"Narada was not an ordinary devotee. He was an advanced saint. He continued to be a singer as wished by him, as he liked to sing the glories of the Lord." The guru replied.

Sudhanva asked, "Guruji, but how could such a great saint stuck in the snares of worldly pleasures?"

"It happens according to the wishes of the Lord, even though it appeared as if the incidents were the workings of some other. In this incident, though Narada cursed the Lord to take such a form, Lord Rama was to take birth as human being to cleanse the world of bad people. That was the celestial plan."

The trek was resumed.

Maruthi asked the guru for one more interesting story. The guru too wanted to pass on nuggets of moral and spiritual principles to help his disciples to shape up into good persons.

So he chuckled in satisfaction and began one more story.

"Once upon a time, that was during the days of Master Buddha, a dacoit used to live in the hills near the place where the Master lived. This dacoit was very cruel and used to cut the fingers of the victims from whom he fleeced off all the valuables they possessed. Any person or group who passed through those hills would invariably become victims of that dacoit. In course of time, people stopped passing through that route and chose another passage way.

His name became byword for cruelty. He was called Angulimal as he used to wear the fingers he cut from his victims as a garland round his neck.

Lord Buddha heard of him. He wanted to reform the dacoit. So one day he set on his journey towards the hills alone. The dacoit saw a lone person approaching the hills. He began chuckling in glee to get another victim so that he could add a few more fingers to his garland. He warned the sanyasi, Master Buddha to go away. But the Master continued his journey. When he came between the two hills, which was the place the dacoit chose to attack, Angulimal jumped before him, with a knife in hand.

But he was not his usual self.

As the Master approached the hills, there was a change in the mind of the dacoit. At first he was astounded at the courage of the person, who even after warning dared to face him, a noted and dreaded dacoit.

The dacoit began losing his cruel temperament as the Master was coming closer to him.

At last he could not but surrender himself before the Master."

The guru stopped his story.

It was past midday and the disciples felt hungry. The guru knew it. All around there were stones and wild bushes. Of course, water was available as springs from the rock formations. But that itself was not enough for survival. They needed something to eat.

The guru said that after a few yards, next to a big boulder and obstructed by it there were some fruit bearing trees. But the disciples could not understand how their guru came to know about those trees, but they believed in him.

When they passed the big boulder, they could really see a number of mango and guava trees full of fruits. They ate them as much as they could and some of them stored in their upper cloth for use later.

The group of mendicants then rested for the night in the comforts of a cave, as usual.

Next day after bathing in the cool springs of the hills, they started on their journey. When the disciples felt for the fruits in the upper cloths, none were found. Each blamed the others for the loss.

The guru smiled and said the fruits of the previous day would not last for the next day. When it becomes necessary, the Lord would provide for them, then and there only.

The disciples then understood that the fruits and trees were there with the blessings of their guru. They then prostrated on the feet of their guru for his compassion for them.

VII

Vacra and his group continued their trek on the eastern side of the mountain. After coming to know they had passed the second camp, they were sure that they need not care the police any more. The police would not venture into those heights.

He asked one of his companion Kali about his last adventure in the town close to which Vacra lived with his family. He liked that incident as the victim was his relative whom he disliked though there was no past enmity with his cousin.

Kali "That was during last summer, boss. You did not like to go with us then."

Vacra "Of course, how could I come to my relative's house? He was my second cousin."

Kali "Boss, they are very rich people."

Vacra "I know, his father was a smuggler. They are traitors."

Kali "Yes boss, we were never like that. We are patriots."

Vacra laughed loudly. His followers enjoyed the joke. They were patriots as they were not smugglers. They only help transfer the wealth of the rich to the poor, in the sense themselves. Of course, now the boss was not poor any more. But that was an exception. But then, there were exceptions for any rule or principle.

Manda said, "Alright, you Kali continue with the story now."

Vacra continued his laughter, "So, why is this fellow so anxious to know about that story?"

And addressing Manda he asked, "Did you not participate in that venture?"

Manda answered with pretentious modesty, "Boss, I was then resting for ten days."

He was in jail where their lodging and boarding needs were taken care of by the authorities.

Vacra burst into laughter once more. Others followed suit.

Kali continued, "Boss, during last summer I and Suri went to your cousin's house in the night. It was two o'clock in the night. We knew there was a watchman at the main gate. So we chose the back side compound wall as the entry point. Suri jumped in first to check and I followed him after a signal from him. Suri used the cutter and opened the backyard door to the kitchen. He went in and I watched from outside. Then unexpectedly the light in the hall was switched on and somebody walked into the kitchen. There were sounds of water trickling into a glass. But there was no sound from Suri. He hid somewhere.

The light was off again. Suri came out and called me in low voice. We waited for some time. Then we entered the bedroom next to the hall, after checking that nobody was sleeping there. We did not hear any sounds outside the house; I mean that of watchman. We thought he must be asleep at that time of night.

Suri who was simply listening to his accomplice till then intervened and said, "Let me continue now. There was a steel cupboard in one corner of the room. I carefully opened that with my master key bunch. We found bundles of currency notes and loaded them into our bags. I kept the door closed so that nobody would make out immediately.

The surroundings were dark but for the dim light of the night lamp. We then headed towards the upstairs portion of the building. We found no light in one of the two bedrooms. From the other one we heard some voices. We waited for some time until the sounds abated. I then carefully opened the door to the bedroom, which was not lit. In one corner there was a wooden cupboard attached to the wall. There was no other cupboard in that room. I signaled to my friend to stay at the door. I opened the door of the cupboard, which was not locked. I was disappointed assuming that no valuables were inside, as the cupboard was open. But I was wrong. Inside the cupboard, I saw in the dim light, one small iron safe riveted to the wooden shelf.

It did not take much time for me to open that safe."

Vacra with a big guffaw, "I know you have become an expert in that. You were trained by whom, else? You must give credit to your boss for that."

Suri at once acknowledged that.

Suri continued, "Inside the iron safe I saw some gold ornaments. I stuffed them into my pockets. I then walked towards the door. We then peeped through the window into the other bedroom which was the only one left.

In our enthusiasm, we both tried to look inside at a time. When the shutter was left to close back it made a creaking sound."

Manda commented anxiously, "You could have left that room alone, having secured so much already."

Vacra shouted loudly, "Shut up. That's not our way of doing things. If you cannot take risk, you can leave us at once."

Manda was frightened and kept his mouth shut with both hands.

Suri resumed, "We at once hid behind the nearby pillar. The light in the room was switched on. A woman came out half naked. She looked around but could not find us."

Then she turned around and while going inside shouted to the person inside the room, "My dear, nobody is here."

Then the other person came out with a bed sheet around his waist."

Kali laughing lightheartedly, "That fellow was a young man in his thirties."

Vacra burst out impatiently, "What are you talking? That fellow I mean my cousin is an old fellow aged around fifty. You could not have seen him properly in the dim light."

He laughed loudly.

Kali continued the narration not noticing the signal of his friend Suri to stop him and said, "Boss that was not her husband. It was somebody else."

Vacra stopped walking, picked a big stone and threw it at Kali in anger. The stone missed its target otherwise Kali would have been maimed or even dead.

He shouted in anger, "How dare you talk like that. I may comment badly about my relatives. But you have no business to take light of our family members. Don't take liberties at that."

He pulled out his revolver and shot two times into the air without aim. One bird which did not expect the sudden violence fell dead at a distance of a few feet.

Vacra a few moments later regained his composure and laughed away the incident.

He encouraged Suri to continue the narration. Suri knew about his boss that was why he did not tell about that adventure in so many details earlier.

Vacra came close to Suri, patted him on the back and said “Alright. Go ahead. Tell me the truth. That cousin of mine, that bugger deserves it right. A smuggler would not be served better by his wife.”

Suri resumed now “But boss that was the truth. Because that lady told the other fellow that he need not be afraid and that her husband would not be home before evening of next day.”

“But unexpectedly I sneezed. A mosquito entered my nose in that dim light. As it was a balcony where we hid, there were many mosquitoes out there. They saw us hid behind the pillar.

The lovers were scared to death. But we having known their relationship were not afraid now.

She shouted in fright “Who are you people and what are you doing here?”

We preferred to keep silent. Then they both walked away into the room in shame.

We too walked out of the house with the bounty without resistance and unharmed.”

Vacra as if talking to himself said, “I don’t know whether I should reveal about the bitch to my dirty cousin or not.”

The trek continued again.

After a few moments a small group of five persons, including two women and a boy of fifteen years appeared before them. They looked frightened. The boy was in fact trembling.

One of the men spoke to the boss, "Sir, we heard some gunshot sounds. Do we encounter any problem now?"

The boss smiled generously and said, "Not immediately. But if you continue on this journey, yes. You better go towards the place from where you came."

He showed them the wrong route to lessen the number of treasure hunters.

After their departure, Kali wondered aloud why they had left them without checking for valuables.

"That treatment is reserved for those who had returned from the top of the mountain. These fellows are still in search of treasures," Vacra said.

They continued their journey. Vacra sensed they came near another camp. Some distant sounds of human presence were audible now.

The boss of the group advised his followers to take possession of all things useful and of necessity from the people residing at the next camp by some means.

Presently they saw some movement of men and women near a village like establishment. There were a number of fruit bearing trees. Some women in dresses like those worn by inmates of an ashram were taking care of the visitors. When Vacra came to one of the hutments, a smiling woman welcomed him.

The residential colony was made up of a number of huts—huts of good quality. They cannot be categorized like those of poor men's dwelling places. Here utility is the basis—utility for night's stay only, as no visitor to these parts would waste time during the day. They were motivated to trek fast on the mountain to reach the top-crest. Those huts were meant to guard the inhabitants against cold and wild animals. They were also made to take care of the privacy of the residents.

Broad leaves of some trees covered on the strong rafters of pine wood, constitute the huts. The leaves were nicely stitched by fibers with long wooden needles.

The ashram woman led Vacra into one of the hutments. Inside the hut the decorations were as eye catching as the exteriors were. He was provided with warm water and vegetable cleaning liquids for washing. He ate nice refreshing meal of forest produce. Later he had a sound sleep having relaxed well with the services rendered to him. When the number was more and accommodation less, the visitors had to compromise with less number of facilities.

Next morning, when the visitors woke up and came out of the shelters they were amazed to watch the beautiful ambience that regaled their senses, the plants with flowers, fruit bearing trees, deer of the forest and so on.

But many of the visitors were in a hurry to move away to the higher regions of the mountain. There was not much time left for enjoyment for them. Perforce they had to stay indoors to take shelter for the unpredictable night. No serious visitor stayed there during the day.

Some others who found the attractions enthralling were reluctant to go away.

However, Vacra and his fellows made haste to get ready to proceed further on their hunt for treasures. They were not new to enjoyments of life. Nobody ever tried to stop them from those joys. They knew still stronger doses of entertainment elsewhere. They were not soft natured to be intoxicated with mild and sensitive treatments of joys of life.

They stuffed their bags with sufficient quantities of fruits and bottles with drinks to last at least for one more day. They were given to understand that some kind or other of food and drink and facility for the night's stay would be available even in the higher camps.

Once on the trek again, Vacra asked his companions while controlling his mirth, as to what material each one of them could secure from other visitors as planned by them in advance. His compatriots looked at each other. They were completely out of their minds, once inside the huts. Moreover, there was no chance of interaction with other visitors there.

Finding them confused to answer Vacra laughed loudly and said, "Alright, I know the occasion was such. Anyway you had refreshed enough now, I think."

He winked at Manda meaningfully, who laughed aloud wholeheartedly.

Other visitors, who too rested in the huts the previous night as did Vacra and his men, were walking behind them at a distance.

Vacra did not like that. He knew that they were competitors in his venture. But he kept his dislike under control for the time being.

After some time he asked Kali whether any useful material could be secured from the fellows coming behind them. Kali looked back keenly and replied some blankets and mattresses were available with those people. They appeared rich. Suri gave a hint that food materials like biscuits and other eatables which town's people eat were there with them. He wanted to tempt his boss to loot them.

Around midday they reached a wide and clear place under the shade of trees. They stopped the trek and spread their mats on the ground there for taking lunch.

Those who were following them too sat next to the group of Vacra. They too opened their bags and began eating.

Now the evening shadows started spreading across. In those parts the sun began setting early.

Vacra aimed and shot a bird dead while it was flying close to them.

At the hint, Kali and Suri went slowly towards the other group. They snatched away the required food materials available there and brought them over to their comrades. Those unfortunate people were aghast, at the sudden incident with surprise and fear. They heard the gun shot and could make out that they were looted by criminals who were ready to shoot to meet their ends.

Vacra and his group ate to their heart's content and got up. In the meantime the visitors of the other group finished their eating fast and were on their way, to avoid mingling with the Vacra group.

However Vacra group closed in and snatched the woolen rugs and mats and other useful things from the dumbfounded other group.

Vacra gave them a warning not to follow them or seen in those parts again, if they want to live longer. Those threatened visitors scattered away from that place. They did not expect that kind of impediment on the way. They were not ready for such threats.

Vacra and his accomplices hastened their steps as it was becoming dark. They should look for some shelter for the night. Vacra looked at his watch. Even after two hours of trek, they did not reach a village.

It was dark already. Saral expressed the doubt that they might have missed the correct route. At a distance, they heard the growling of wild animals. Vacra assured his companions they need not be afraid as they were well armed. As if to test the revolver and also to scare away any approaching animals, he aimed at a rabbit moving at a distance and fired a shot. It fell dead. Before they could lay their hands on it, a jackal or some predator-animal snatched it away. They could not clearly see what that animal was.

Now Vacra became vigilant. It was clear by that incident that wild animals were not scared of gunshot sounds when they were hungry. He asked his men to climb on to the high tree branches to save themselves from the animals. But tall trees were very few there.

All of them dispersed to different treetops at different places. The boss told his men not to sleep that night. Vacra and another man settled on a tree.

They heard the growls and roars of wild animals now and then. After some time they saw animals prowling near the trees. They might have got the scent of human beings. Now it was doubly clear that unless they were alert they could be in irretrievable dangers.

Vacra and others were jolted into wakefulness from the short slumber, when they heard the cry of one of the men and then a thud sound as if somebody had fallen down. One of the men in the group fell down from the tree. He tried to climb up another tree. The tree on which he sat was attacked by wild-ants. There was an ant nest below the tree where he was stationed previously. Manda who was close to that tree poured water from the bottle on him, so that ants could leave him. Then he burnt the leaves around him with matches to scare them away. Before another attack, he quickly climbed the tree where Manda was and he could save himself.

* * *

Vacra and his men were on trek once more by the time the sun was up in the sky. They were exhausted by the previous night's experiences. Before noon, they sighted some signs of a village at a distance.

After reaching the village, they found it a well-planned group of houses for visitors. Around the village, there were cultivated lands. Some householders during their vanaprastha ashramam period arranged for visitors to reside for night halt. Another visitor who happened to pass them explained about the ashramams to Vacra in short.

By tradition, Indian householders observed four stages during the length of their life.

It starts with the boyhood stage called Brahmacharya. In this period the boy was sent to a teacher and stays with him till he completes his education. All the needs of the boy were taken care of by the teacher. The education comprises of certain sastras, which are codified knowledge field-wise, for example, finance or arthasastra. After completion of studies, the boy's father offer some gifts or money to the teacher. There was no compulsion however for this.

Grihastasram comes after the Brahmacharya. The boy who reached adulthood gets married and leads a house-holders life.

When the house-holder completes discharging his duties, he becomes fit for the next ashram which goes by the name Vanaprastha. In this stage he hands over the responsibilities of the house and business or lands to his offspring and goes into the forests with his wife to lead a life in search of spiritual fulfillment.

After a life of Vanaprastha, the final stage is called Sanyasa ashramam. The individual abandons even the few facilities he enjoyed in the previous ashramam and becomes a sanyasi. He would not have any relationship with family members. He lives on the food offered by others and sleeps at the places where he happens to be on his sojourn.

The villagers provided all visitors including Vacra and his group, rotis and vegetable side dishes. The visitors had a nice meal.

After meal, one of the visitors from other than Vacra group began entertaining them with anecdotes and stories.

He began the story with words, "To keep you engaged and till you get sleep, I will tell you a story."

He moved close to the wall, wall of the front hall-like thatched structure of the main hutment and reclined against it. It appeared obviously a long story.

Vacra on a close look at that person recognized him to be one of those whom they had looted the previous day. When Vacra was looking at him, that man whose name it was given to be Siladhara, was watching Suri of Vacra group with keen interest. After the stranger turned his gaze away, Vacra bent towards Kali who was next to him and told him his doubt. He asked him to pass on the information to others of his group, so that they would be ready for any eventuality.

Siladhara continued "During my childhood days, in our village there were two close friends well known for their selfless friendship. Viswam was a rich land-owner and his friend Narasu was a poor school teacher in the same village. Viswam used to try to help his friend with money and materials. But Narasu was very self-respecting and refused any help from his friend. He explained to his friend that money should not be a hindrance for their friendship and that he should not misunderstand his refusal. Each of them had a son and they taught them to be friends like themselves.

But both the children were not good at studies. They were always engaged in playing and mischief making. Their parents pampered them and the result was that in due course of time they became slaves to bad habits.

Viswam's son Marthanda used to provide all the requirements of Narasu's son Vikram. Marthanda used to wear valuable diamond rings on all the five fingers of his right hand. Vikram had only a silver one on one finger. On one occasion in raised tempers, he challenged his friend and said that one day he will excel Marthanda in wearing valuables.

Marthanda in lighter vein asked his friend "How will you do that? Will you wear rings on the toes too or what?"

Vikram did not reply. He was thinking deeply.

The boys grew up as spendthrifts and beyond reforming.

Before they passed their teen age, fathers of the two boys died with lingering worries about their unsuccessful sons. After the death of fathers, their spoiled sons became free and in no time they spent away all the money they had.

During one severe summer, mother of Marthanda died. On the third day of that incident, both friends discussed during the whole night. They had to plan for their future so as to live happily.

Vikram left his mother with his grandparents explaining them that he was going to the nearby town for securing a job. The grandparents knew about his ways and did not believe his words. However they could not do anything to change him.

Then the two friends took steps to sell their houses and other properties. It was not difficult for them to sell away the properties. They were not aware of the prevailing prices and the method of negotiation. They did neither approach well-wishers for help. They were in a hurry to convert the properties into cash, to get away from that place and enjoy their lives.

With the money secured by the sale of properties, they started on their journey to another town. For security of money and themselves, each of them carried a knife usually kept for security in the houses."

At this point Vacra laughed loudly.

All the eyes were turned to them. The narrator asked him whether there was any mistake in his description or he did not like the story.

Vacra had to reply.

He said controlling his laughter now, "What good it would be to carry the knives when they never had an occasion to use them?"

The narrator, reigning in his anger against the interrupter said, "That we will know in later part of the story."

Vacra recollected the incident in which the rich householder who held a license for the gun could not use it when he was attacked by Vacra group. That was a decade back. It was a revolver that man tried to fire at Vacra. They had filled their bags with many of the valuables picked in the house by then. The house owner was asleep keeping full faith on his watchman's capability. The watchman was overpowered in no time by Vacra's men. The watchman had never encountered a determined attacker till then. When they hit him pitiless, he begged for their mercy. They tied him with a rope which was provided by that man only.

When they were leaving the place, the house owner appeared on the scene, with his revolver. He aimed at Vacra alright, but could not pull the trigger. He was thinking of the harm that will befall on the other and his hand was shaking like a leaf in the gust of wind. Vacra took away the revolver with no effort from him and made it his own.

He touched the revolver kept safely under his belt. That brought him another satisfied laughter.

The story teller looked at him in disgust and with impotent anger.

He continued the narration, "They crossed their village and by evening entered the neighboring town. They stayed for the night in a rented accommodation. They ate nice meal for the first time away from home. As they were tired very much, they slipped into deep sleep as soon as they were on the beds. At midnight, two thieves who had been watching them entered the room by cutting the rods of the window. They took away the money pouches. One of the thieves saw the diamond rings shining on the fingers of Marthanda. He pulled away the rings while the other forced the hands of the victim down. The victim woke up and tried to recover his loved rings. With his cries, his friend too woke up. Vikram in a quick move pulled out the knife from his bag and attacked one of the thieves. He gave a loud cry and fell down. The second thief snatched away the other's bag too. He then jumped through the window and escaped away.

When the two friends looked at the injured thief, he was bleeding and motionless. He might be dead.

With the happening of the sudden violent incident, they were scared and could not bear the sight. Thinking of the consequences, they ran away from the spot at once.

By the time the sunrays were out, they were far away from the dreaded spot. They cleaned away the blood marks from their clothes and changed into another set. By mid-day they reached another town. They satisfied their hunger by buying food stuff with the money left over with them. All the money they brought with them was stolen away by the thief. Now they had to earn money to live, for their daily requirement of food, shelter and other expenses.

They discussed about the methods of earning money. They had no skills to use. They never thought of that. They were neither good in business. Moreover, there was no capital to start any business.

Marthanda suggested that they should earn money by some means to start with, in the sense by good method or bad. Once they had capital, they could start some business and earn thereafter by fair means.

They both discussed at length again on that. At last, they concluded that theft was the easiest and fast method to secure capital. At that moment, a marriage procession with all the paraphernalia was passing on the road opposite to them. Marthanda said at once that a mass-theft at the marriage function was safe and that it gives a large capital at one stroke for the proposed business venture.

They waited for such a suitable opportunity for a long time. They managed in the mean time with one meal a day, taking shelter under a roadside verandah.

During the course of their trips around the town, one day they saw at one place, arrangements for marriage performance. That place was well suited for their purpose.

That was a secluded place, making it safe for easy escape. On enquiry, they found that the time of the marriage was in the night. That too suited them well.

They discussed about the method of operation-theft. When venturing into a big crowd of people as that of a marriage, unless they show their superior power they cannot make the people obey to their diktats. That means though they were two in number, they must be able to threaten the crowd effectively. Otherwise, they could be overpowered and beaten. That was possible only with the show of firearms, but not with the knives they had. They should have guns, small or big ones.

Marthanda suggested that the guns could be those used for shooting the birds, air guns. They won't kill people. It releases pellets, which will cause injuries. As their intention was to threaten and bring them under control, air guns would suffice. Vikram agreed to that. With the sound of gun—of course they would fire in the air—the crowd would be scared and they could ask them to remove their valuables and hand them over. Then they would go away as fast as they came with the booty and guns.

But that gun had to be purchased. They did not have the wherewithal for that. Vikram said they would get it from some firearm shop in the night. They might not be able to avoid this small kind of burglary, for once. After that, they could start their business with that money. They made a mental picture of their later life and became jubilant.

With youthful exhilaration, Marthanda punched the air with his fist. They shook hands in happiness for the good days to come.

They should get the weapons that night only as the marriage was scheduled for the next night.

They had a sparse meal, which only they could afford and started for survey of the shops—arms shops. In the market where they sell hardware, at the end of the row, two arms shops were nestled side by side. They passed in front of the shops looking at the arms displayed in the glass cases. Small arms like revolvers and handguns were only visible from outside. Vikram commented to his friend that he felt like taking away one of those guns. He liked them. Air guns were not there. He suggested going into the shop, for enquiry about their availability. But on second thought, they desisted from that idea. Why should they give an opportunity for anybody to recognize them in case of an adversity?

They could select weapons best suited for their purpose later in the night. There was no alternative other than those two shops for them. The weapons would wait for them to choose.

They postponed the matter for that night.

Marthanda expressed doubt there might be night watchman on rounds. So they should take that into consideration and go to the shop when he had passed that street.

Vikram suggested they should use torch light for looking for the guns. They should not give scope for doubts by putting the electric lights on.

They bought a torch light that evening at the road side shop for a low price. They didn't have enough money to purchase a fanciful light."

Vacra and his men were listening to the storyteller keenly, to note if any useful hints emerge from the story. At one stage, Vacra suspected that the storyteller aimed at them in telling this kind of story and wanted to wait till the end to know how he would conclude it.

Manda was trying to remember how they acquired their arms. That was five years back. They were getting away from a police party chasing them. They had finished a heist in a new colony of houses that came up on the outskirts of Agra. They were five including the boss at that time. In the hurry they entered one of the villages close to Chambal. When they passed the village they saw a thug's body next to the high earthen formation beyond the boundary. At some distance, another body was lying. Each of the deceased had two guns, one in hand gripped tightly another in holster, a revolver. They picked all of them. Boss said they died during inter gang encounters. He gave the arms to them, for future use.

The narrator resumed after stretching himself to a more comfortable position, "The two friends, when every household was asleep, walked towards the market place. At the end of the street a lone dog barked at them. The night watchman who heard that made sounds with his stick on the ground to get rid of the daily nuisance. He did not see the two friends going on errand. They took care to avoid him as planned before.

Vikram remembered his grandmother's words never to respond or care barking dogs. They were a hindrance to progress and they were jealous about the successful. Ignore them, his Grandmother told. Obviously, it was a reference to the humans.

They now reached the arms shops and chose the bigger one. Nobody was in sight. With the help of the torch, they could locate the latch on which the padlock was secured. Marthanda began cutting the latch with help of the hacksaw, while his friend kept a watch on the street. The guard would not be on this side until some time. Before that, they had to finish their work.

Once the door was open, they went in and closed the door back from inside. They looked for the air guns. But such arms could not be located anywhere. There was not much time to waste. So, they grabbed two revolvers and sufficient ammunition. They now heard vigil sounds of the watchman at far end of the street. They closed the door and left it as it was before the theft, so that nobody could notice any change. They came out without waste of time after checking for any unexpected intruders. The duo walked away by the other end of the street towards their residence. They slept well after their arduous first theft.

Marthanda and Vikram spent the next day planning and modifying the method of operation-theft of that night. They were nervous thinking about the operation, which was to be done in the glare of all those assembled for the marriage. Previous night's theft was different as it was carried out in the dark, without the notice of anybody. They prayed to God for success of the operation. The owner of the shop too might have prayed for the safety of his merchandise. God probably ensures the solution of the paradox by granting the desire of the more sincere of the two.

During the course of the sparse midday meal, they buttressed their resolve with the thought that instead of suffering with half-filled stomachs and poor quality of the food, its better taking the risk and getting sufficient money to live happily. By pondering about theft on those lines, they also lessened the burden of the misdeed and consequent fear and nervousness. They contemplated about the plan once more lest they miss the finer details.

The final plan, which they agreed to, was like this- Marthanda would go first to the place of marriage in the evening. That was situated amongst buildings of the new township at the eastern end of the town. He was to find whether any second gate was there, other than the main gate in case of necessity. Was it possible to climb over the compound wall? How big would be the congregation? That he could assess by the number of chairs placed there."

At this point somebody in the listeners commented with a loud laughter, "I didn't know that even for theft, such a detailed plan is necessary."

Siladhara, the narrator replied with a smile and a passing glance towards Vacra, "You may not know, but some others may be well versed."

It was like a provocation. But Vacra did not respond. He would take care of the fellow later, he reflected grudgingly. One or two of his followers too understood the comment of the narrator and what it purported to mean.

The narrator continued, "They have to operate at the dais. The marriage parties would be preparing in the rooms attached to the dais on either side. So, the passage from the dais to the gate and its distance must be known in advance.

They have to walk towards the dais an hour before the time of marriage. Marriage was to take place at nine in the night. They have to conceal faces with the masks before firing the shot into the air to scare them. They wear the masks after reaching the dais. Taking advantage of the surprise element, they would grab the money, valuables, and stuff them in the bags each of them carry. Obviously, they would not give time for any of the assembled to think and act.

After finishing the operation, they walk out, remove the masks and escape in different routes. They would meet at the railway station. From there, they could go away to some distant town by the first train arriving on the platform. Once the masks were removed they would become gentlemen like any other passengers waiting for the train.

At around eight in the evening, the two friends armed with the tools proceeded to the place of marriage function. After waiting for a few minutes in the hall, they walked towards the dais.

When they were a few feet away to the dais, suddenly the lights were off. There was a power break down. It was an unexpected hindrance.

They sat down amongst the invitees and waited there. The power supply was resumed after a few minutes, luckily for them. God was on their side in this operation-theft.

After that, there was no looking back. The operation went on as planned. The crowd did not resist. There were no cell phones in those days. Even if they were there, you cannot expect the police to arrive at the right time to catch the thieves and get injured in the process. There was no chance for them to get injuries in this case. It was always safer and better to come leisurely. There was nothing to lose for them personally.

The marauders fired two shots into the air. The assemblage became still and silent.

So the duo while pointing the guns at the crowd walked away through the main gate only. After going out into the street they removed the masks and went by different routes to the railway station. There was nobody to accost them. There was nobody on the road in that remote area, at that time of the night.

After some time they both met at the station."

The listeners heaved a sigh of relief. Somebody sighed loudly indicating the boredom.

The narrator looked at him and said, "I am also feeling sleepy. I will close the story within a short time."

He continued, "They waited for the arrival of a train. They laughed away while discussing about the operation and how simple it turned out to be in the end. They were even tempted to plan another such operation instead of going for a business venture, success of which was not certain.

Time passed on, but the train did not arrive. Then two persons in khaki uniform came to the place where the friends were sitting, from behind the bench. They sat next to them. One of them asked Marthanda where they were going.

He could not answer at once. The friends were scared now. Both the intruders were bulky and appeared to be taking plenty of food and rest since many years. They suspected them to be police men.

The second person asked him what was that he was carrying in the bag. He replied that they were his clothes and they were going to his grandmother's place.

The policemen then pulled away the bags from them and checked in side. The theft was out. The two thieves tried to escape but could not.

So much for the bad ways of the wicked and the story ends there."

Siladhara thanked the listeners and got to his feet.

After the story session they dispersed to their allotted places to sleep.

Vacra addressing his fellows said, "This fellow was eying me a number of times. He recognized us. But what do I care? Even now, I can finish him. Nobody would come to his rescue in these mountain ranges."

Another of the group said angrily, "Boss, he wantonly ended the story with the incident wherein thieves were caught by the police. Does he want to scare us or what?"

Another said "What they can do to us? We were caught by the police many times. What is the harm? They are like our friends only. We have our ways of dealing with them."

Vacra said, "Okay, we will deal with him later. We may meet him again somewhere on this mountain."

His associates laughed loudly visualizing the scene of punishment meted out to the narrator of the story.

VIII

Charudas slowed his pace of walk. He appeared tired. It was not physical exhaustion. He was thinking and working on his writings.

As they go to higher regions, the food taken became less. It was not cooked food. They had to satisfy themselves with fruits and roots only. They did not feel the necessity of eating more. The terrain was not steep now. It looked almost flat. They were not exerting much, it might be due to the topography or the nature of the ambience was such.

Charudas had been jotting down notes on the sheaf of papers, which he carried wherever he went. He expressed his satisfaction over the progress he made in writing.

When he saw somebody and recollected some incident pertaining to a person similar to him from his acquaintances in his own life, he began weaving a story around him and that society. Or when he encountered a scene or beauties of nature, he might get inspiration and would be prompted into action. Some times when his spirits were lifted up with lofty ideas, his mind floats into poetic temperament and a nice poem snuggled on to the paper.

Sudhama had been talking to Nishit of the essence of good life and various methods for circumventing the tragedies one may come across in life. Nishit was open-minded and he liked the advices of Sudhama. He accepted the latter's integrity and simplicity. He believed that Sudhama was sincere in helping him.

Veera asked Charudas the writer, "Sir, you have been writing so much all these days. We could make out from the bundles of papers you carry. If the subject is interesting please read out for us what you wrote."

Sharad seconded him.

"Sir, are you writing stories? If so please let us share the joy of hearing them. Other than stories, I am not interested." He pleaded.

Chandra looked at him with curiosity. Sharad fascinated her. She tried to compare him with Veera, her husband. She was disappointed in the process.

Charudas glanced around. There were more than two dozen eyes staring at him in eagerness, eagerness born out of boredom. They had abandoned their usual activities which they were accustomed to at their places, for the sake of this visit. The routine of trekking, eating, resting and again trekking took away the charm of life. It had become a mechanical life. There was no novelty here. Some of them even began doubting the availability of the treasures atop the mountain. However they could not abandon the venture and return home, for fear of mockery it evokes in their own near and dear, in addition to the loss of money spent by them until then. Nevertheless the enthusiasm on the faces of others, rekindled their hopes.

It was past midday. They ate the fruits they brought from previous resting place. There were many water pools though the water was cold. However, they had to satisfy themselves with that.

Charudas sat with his back rested against the trunk of the tree under which they assembled now. The ground was clear, might be due to the climatic conditions of the higher regions. As it was past spring time trees bore light green leaves in abundance. The visitors sat around Charudas facing him. They sat on the bed sheets and fiber-mats they brought with them, to make themselves comfortable on the bare ground.

Charudas looked up to see the canopy of the green leaves above. One or two birds as if they shared the enthusiasm of their human counter parts below, watched the scene from up there.

He saw at the people assembled around—a dozen weather beaten and yet enthusiastic faces.

He smiled and began, "My friends, we have been together for a few weeks in this testing trek. Though we were with each other for not much time, we had become like a close- knit family. We faced the trials and tribulations together with the common aim. Some of us may be losing the enthusiasm with which they started on this journey. But I request you all not to think in terms of distrust, distrust about the possibility of achievement or other things.

One of the visitors who was impatient of this long introduction, asked him to begin the story he wrote.

The writer smiled again and said, "I know, you are eager to hear something new. Some of us had turned on the radios we brought without any success. We are cut off even from our friends and relatives, as we are beyond the places where phones work.

But we know we are far ahead of others on this journey. We have crossed the third camp and close to fourth one.

All right, now reverting to the story—in fact—it is not a story—it is a real incident or chain of incidents.

During my school days, I had two friends in the same class with me. There was no school in our village. We three used to travel a few miles every day to reach the school.

One of the two friends Ranjit belonged to a rich family of landowners. He travelled in a car to reach the school. Karan and I used to go to school on a bicycle owned by

Karan. My father was a school teacher at another village. He could not afford to maintain well our family of four—father, mother myself and my younger brother.

Karan's father was in government service. He used to earn extra income by other means.

Though Ranjit was rich, he used to be friendly to us. Once he took us to town in his car. We three went to a hotel and then to a movie.

I would tell the hotel incident to show how the mind of a criminal works.

We ate some snacks. The supplier boy gave us the bill. In those days, pens were rare and costly. Pencils were used by common people. The bill was scribbled by a pencil. We were to go to the cashier to pay the bill. Karan pulled out a pencil from his pocket and changed the figure to a lower amount—it was thirty made to twenty, I think. We two being young succumbed to his mischief, though tried to refrain him in the beginning. Ranjit paid twenty and we came out without any trouble. We had a hearty laugh at the expense of the cashier.

Our next program was to go to a movie. Before that we made a trip to the town. It was interesting for us from village, to watch the town and its residents once in every few months. We were enthused with their un-crumpled dresses and brisk movements. In village, the local folk take things leisurely and everything takes its own time.

By the time we reached the theatre, booking was closed. We could only buy tickets at double the rates in black market—that means from the fellows who purchased tickets to sell for profit. The theater owners themselves encourage that to get a cut from the touts. What we gained at the hotel we lost at the theater.

When we were in tenth class, Karan became school leader, with the monetary support of Ranjit. His father though earned much did not pamper his son. But, Karan could get things whatever he wanted on credit because of his father's position.

One evening, I saw him behind the park with a girl. The girl was crying. I heard her saying, "Please don't desert me."

We went on a picnic to a beautiful spot near the neighboring town, a hillock with a lake on top. A fort of erstwhile kings was in a dilapidated condition on it. Ranjit drove his car to that place. The car could go up to some height. After that, we trekked up the hill. There were large banyan trees, monkeys hanging on their branches. It was all wild growth. We saw a large snake creeping into a crevice as we entered the fort. On the first floor of the fort a magnificently decorated—decorated in limestone carvings-durbar hall was there. We could imagine the erstwhile durbar gathering watching a soulful song-dance, as in the Moghul-e-ajam movie. We ate our lunch on the terrace of that hall, under the cool shade of a tree. We knew that the water in the lake was safe to drink.

Before it was dark, we were on return journey.

We saw a big crowd just before entering the town we lived in. A girl was dead and a boy in his teens was nearby, held by a policeman. The place was close to the hostel for the mentally retarded boys. We learnt that boy who was from that hostel killed the girl after raping her. That was the version of the police, but the men gathered there were not inclined to believe that. They argued that someone raped and killed her and after killing left the body close to the hostel. That innocent boy seen near the body was trapped in that crime, by mistake or conveniently by somebody that killed her, nobody knew.

As Ranjit stopped the car, we got down to find out why the crowd gathered there. Karan remained behind and did not want to see the 'horrible incident'.

When I went near the body and saw the face, I recognized her as the same girl who was with Karan and crying behind the park, a few days back.

I asked Karan pulling him aside, "Do you know her?"

He denied knowing her, at once.

Karan and Ranjit went to college after finishing the high school study in the town. I stopped studies due to lack of financial support.

I did not meet my friends for a long time. However, I met Karan after more than a decade. In the meantime, I had shifted to Mumbai for getting a job. I joined a private firm as a clerk. I was married and stayed on the outskirts of the city. I used to travel by local train to go to office and back.

While in the private service, I began writing short stories and send them to some journals. They were published. I continued to write and authored a few books in course of time. And some books were acclaimed.

Once while I was travelling by train, I saw Karan in a car at the railway crossing. He looked rich.

My neighbors in the compartment talked about him as a rich realtor. They criticized him for his ruthless ways of acquiring land. He occupied government lands with the help from politicians and officials. He took away lands that were in disputes and of those who could not defend their titles. He became rich by wrong means.

After several years, I had honed myself into a good writer. One of my books was selected for award. On the awards day, I was invited to be on the dais. On the dais, I found none other than Karan by my side. He garlanded me and the chairman gave me the award. Karan recognized me and introduced me to the chairman as his friend.

Karan spoke a few words with me and appreciated my talent. He gave his visiting card and asked me to see him at the address he wrote on the back of the card.

On a convenient day I went to him. He waited for me with a lady who I thought was his wife. But he said she was his close friend and he lived with her too. I was embarrassed and felt it as a dishonor. Nobody would call a friend to his paramour's house for honoring or showing his affection.

He entertained me with food and drink. At the time of leaving, he asked me to dedicate my next book to him. I could guess how calculating he was.

At this point of narration, Sharad interrupted Charudas.

"My dear sir, this is all your autobiography. How can this be a story? If you have any short stories evoking fun or romantic stories in your kit please do us the favor of reading them."

Charudas burst into laughter and said, "All right. Now I know you are not interested in this. We will postpone this to some other day. Now I will switch over to a different subject."

All those assembled laughed at the exchange between them. Charudas thought that there was a discernible change in their moods.

The narrator began "Now another story—the time was nine in the evening—first show of the movie was over. Viewers made a line to the bus stop which was a few steps away. When the bus arrived, they pushed in, to occupy the vacant seats at once. Others hanged on to the overhead leather straps for support. The short tube lights emitted enough light for the conductor to issue tickets. The bus moved away from the crossroads and took a left turn towards the university road. At the first stop, half the bus became vacant. At the next bus-stop, many more got down. The bus was moving on. No other passengers got in, after that. A middle-aged couple and a teenaged girl with them and a few others continued their journey. Out of the few others, two young boys began taunting the young girl, wedged between her parents. The conductor did not bother. He was immersed in filling his daily schedules.

After some time the two boys aged twenty plus, moved close to the seat where the girl and parents sat. The father of the girl took objection and threatened them with a complaint to the police. But they had not changed their attitude. At this point, the conductor spared a moment to advice the bad boys to stop their antics. But they did not heed.

Another boy of the same age who was in the bus and had been a witness to this, got up from his seat and went to the bad boys. He warned them. They retaliated by pushing him back. At the jerk of the bus, he fell down on the floor of the bus. At once, he got up and hit the other two on the stomachs very hard. They took a moment to absorb the shock. Then they jumped on the lone savior and began hitting him.

Now, unexpectedly the parents of the girl joined the good boy in attacking the bad ones. Those two did not expect this sudden onslaught. They only knew that the victims always were coerced into inaction out of fear. It was new to see them retaliate. As the bus was going slowly, the two bad boys jumped out to save grace. The conductor now found time to laud the good boy for his bold action. He opined that if people act so boldly against mischief-makers, such incidents would not occur.

Some days later, the good boy, named Sachin went to the market. He bought some household necessities and was on his way back home. Two boys of same age pounced on him from a side lane. With the sudden attack, Sachin fell flat on the footpath. His bagful of purchases were strewn everywhere.

Sachin got to his feet and began hitting his assailants with use of martial art techniques. The two bad boys could not fight him back. They guessed as they were two they could over power Sachin easily. However, to their surprise Sachin began using karate techniques. They ran away after some unsuccessful defense.

Sachin had learnt martial arts—Karate and Kung-Fu with seriousness after the incident in the bus; he learnt the martial arts by putting forth extra efforts.

After earning the black belt and so on, he started free classes for young aspirants. He became popular in his locality.

He was good in studies too. He got an engineering degree and became a civil engineer."

Now one of the listeners asked the narrator, "This does not sound like a story. Anyway where is Sachin now?"

There were smiles all over.

Charudas said "He lives now in my town only. He is an engineering consultant."

Sharad asked, "How do you know him and about those incidents? Is he related to you, sir?"

Charudas with a big guffaw, "Yes, I know him well because he is my son."

The entire area resounded with their guffaws. A bird on the tree fluttered away in confusion, clipping down a few fresh leaves on the way.

IX

The group of Vacrathunda, that was his full name, now reached a nice level ground. It was a bright morning.

They found a lake full of crystal-clear water on the way. They smelt bad to each other of the stinking sweat, with the continuous journey of two days. The vision of a water body like that was there in their minds already, as they needed a bath badly.

Vacra gave orders for a halt. The burglars, they were so, undressed one by one and jumped at different places of the lake. The lake gave no particular choice for a place to enter, as all around it was a level ground. They could take a leap anywhere they liked.

They played in the water like children. They swam to their heart's content. Water was clean and they drank it. They began the process of cleaning every part of their dirty bodies.

On one side of the lake, however, there was a small rock formation. Hidden in between the rocks were a couple of crocodiles. One of them stealthily slipped towards the water. However, as there was not sufficient camouflage, one amongst the group saw it, though at the last moment of its entry into the water.

There was panic everywhere. Once in water the croc was very swift. It headed towards the nearest person. It was Saral. Saral was a thin person and he swam hastily towards the bank and escaped the croc. Vacra was the next to reach the bank and he at once laid his hands on the revolver. He cocked it ready for shooting.

In the meantime unnoticed by them, the second croc neatly slithered into the water. The last to come out was Manda and he was close to the large snout of the second croc in inches. Others who watched that shouted in fear. Vacra who was ready gave a sure shot. The croc at once reversed its path. Manda reached the shore.

On the way where there were bushes and wild grass, they hunted. They could secure food by hunting, whenever they missed a shelter and food on the way.

By evening, they neared a camp. They could make out that when they saw a number of huts at a distance. They began walking briskly now.

Manda wanted to relieve himself and went behind a boulder beside the path. Another followed him. Manda while looking back at him stepped on the tail of a snake which was lying there. That snake was already injured and immobile. It was a poisonous snake and it bit its fangs into him.

Manda shouted in pain first and when he saw the snake, he became mad with fear. He howled so loud his companions were scared. Saral and another brought him away from the boulder and tried to save him by making a cut at the place of bite and removing the poison. But he did not show signs of recovery and was in unconscious state. Then they carried him on a stretcher made of bamboo sticks. After reaching the village, they sought help from the villagers. But it was late by then and Manda could not survive. His body turned bluish. He breathed his last there in that village.

His body was cremated on the outskirts of that village with the help of the villagers. His colleagues wept bitterly over the loss. They pitied him for his misfortune as he only was subjected to one calamity after another.

That whole night, they spent in recollecting the incidents involving Manda. They collected whatever valuables he had on him at the time of death, to be handed over to his wife later.

Vacra was not his usual self. He was distressed at the loss of one of his long time fellows.

During the course of conversation, they came to know that place was called third camp. They had two more camps to pass to reach the top one. They were happy for having passed three camps and at the same time sad to have lost a colleague.

Vacra reconciled to the fate of his colleague after pondering for some time. His usual cruel temperament took over.

So now, for Vacra it was some work done by providence to lessen the number of shares on the treasure. He pondered over that and counted the number now remaining. It was seven now, including himself. He regretted for bringing with him all of his followers. He could have stopped some telling them that the treasures would be distributed as was done with the loot on earlier occasions. Nobody would have objected. Who could dare to object? Moreover, they had faith in him.

Next morning Vacra and his party of six now, began their journey once again. They packed some food and carried water for use in the noon.

His companions however were unhappy over the death of Manda. He was a source of fun with his antics and foolish talk and deeds. He was not mindful of the fun made at his expense, as he knew others enjoyed it. He was broadminded enough to ignore it. They talked about him. Saral said he felt as if a bolt is thrust into his heart whenever he thought of Manda.

Vacra wanted to make his followers active once again, by diverting their attention from the tragedy of the death of Manda.

He motioned to Saral to come near him and asked, "This trip was sudden and unexpected. We took this course of action after your visit to the ashram and on the advice of the swami. Suppose this was not to happen, Saral what would have been our program?"

The burglars began thinking. They did not remember that program at once. Some of them were not informed then, about the future-plans.

Vacra became impatient. He wondered how that small tragedy made his companions ineffective. They had become vegetables, without proper challenges to face.

However, Saral was the first to recollect.

He replied with a smile, "Boss we were to visit a bank."

"That was not a visit. We are not visitors to banks. We are V.I.P's, man. They would be shaken to receive us. Ours is a surprise visit. They cannot reject or avoid it." Vacra boasted.

Suri said after he was a given signal to talk by Vacra.

"Boss, I remember now clearly. We were to hire the building next to that bank for one year as the owner refused to let it out for a few months as required by us."

Shyama took over, "Boss, we had paid that owner two month's rent as advance. That was ten thousands. We have to recover that from him. We did not use that house even for one day."

Vacra thoughtfully, "Yes, we have to recover from him, after reaching the town. But why that house for rent and all that?"

He pretended as if he was not aware of that program. He wanted his men to go back to those days mentally. They were fully active with one assignment after another in those days. They were all busy with the intelligent planning and operation of various programs by their boss. Vacra had been in that business since he was a child.

"Boss, we had planned to make a tunnel underground from that building to the treasure chest in the bank. But after this program, we changed our plans." Suri resumed.

"So, that building is still under our lease only. If necessary, we may continue with our plans later." Vacra declared. He was being playful so that his followers would regain their enthusiasm in action.

"But boss, with this grand treasure at our disposal, is it necessary to go ahead with the old plans?" asked Shyama.

Vacra thoughtfully again, "We don't know the future. You have seen the death of Manda. This is a new type of venture. I am not discouraging you people. But here after, take care before you do anything, particularly in new places."

Vacra laughed loudly as if it was a joke to clear the gloomy atmosphere. All his colleagues joined him.

Vacra gave the war cry with great energy, "Now, attack the treasure trove at the top. Don't lose heart. We had started on this journey with the sole purpose of looting the treasures and make our life easier later on. It's like a war. We may lose some amongst us. But the treasures will reach the families of all. After all, we all worked together. It is fair and just to take care of the families of those died on the way. Jai Bhavani!"

All of them joined him and shouted loudly, "Jai Bhavani!"

Now that appeared to rouse some enthusiasm in them. They recollected the purpose of that arduous journey. The thought of treasures at the top of the mountain rekindled their spirits. Yes, what the boss said was right. They cannot leave the job half done. The benefits will reach all. It would not matter, if some of them died, they thought.

Vacra looked at his colleagues and a smile crossed his face. In case all of them die, it would not matter, as long as he saved himself. But some must live till he reached the base of the mountain, after acquiring the treasures. He needed some guards to defend from any enemy. He thought, as he planned some others might be planning too. So guards he must have. But how many should be there? That time will decide. He left that to future. Of course, he would revise the plan as required at that time.

They began walking with a new gait now. Shyama entertained a doubt. That was nagging him since many days. His doubt was how much each one of them would get after they lay their hands on the treasure trove. Of course, he knew his boss's share would be higher and he would not mind it. He itched to find out from his boss now as the boss was in a good mood. Of course, he promised shares even to the families of the dead.

Shyama asked the boss with a grin across his face, "Boss, if you don't mind could I know what share each one could get from the treasure?"

Boss smiled wickedly. At once the burglar gang was stiffened with fear. Shyama regretted asking that question.

But Vacra pondered over his own situation as he assessed a few moments before. He needed their co-operation.

So he said benignly after some thought, “We are eight persons including the share of Manda. But as I am boss I should get more, what do you say?”

He wanted to find out each one’s mind on that issue. At least, he could judge their mentality in times of such adverse situation.

Saral said knowing his boss’s mind, “Boss, you should get half the share. Balance only to us. You are the leader and guiding spirit to us.”

None others spoke after that categorical sanction. After being asked again, they all said they were of the same opinion. The boss thanked them for their generosity and said that they could decide that when they get that treasure. After all, they were all together in thick and thin.

It was midday. They were tired now. It was time for after noon meal. Whatever they brought from the previous camp, they unfastened the packets and began eating.

There was some shuffling sound from a distance. Within moments, a group of four appeared near them. They begged for food.

Vacra asked the first person who approached him.

“Where are you going?”

“We are going to the top of the mountain.”

With a smile he continued, “I think you are also going there.”

Vacra got angry for his audacity. However he controlled himself. Now after the death of Manda, he became mellowed in behavior. It was necessary till the work was finished.

“Yes, that is right, I too guess so.” Vacra said.

He then asked his companions to share some food with the newcomers. Saral and others were surprised to notice the change in the behavior of their boss.

One of the new comers asked, "Sir, why are you saying so? Do you have any other options?"

"Yes, I guess we have limited options and take things as they happen. Because we never know what will happen the next moment in these parts. It is very uncertain. Yesterday only one of our companions died of snake bite," Vacra replied.

"Of course, in this hill region snakes cannot be avoided. We have medicines for that. We came prepared."

"If you could spare some, please give us."

"Certainly, why not? You are kind enough to share food with us in this desolate place."

He opened his bag and gave some roots and powder to Vacra.

"These roots are available here too. Such plants could be located here in this wild place. The powder is of the same roots. This powder has to be taken in with water and the roots touched at the place of bite."

He then took Vacra some feet away and after some search located that plant. He plucked and showed the leaves to identify the plant.

After finishing the meal, they all started on the trek again.

By evening they reached a village. All of them rested for the night there. They cooked some food with the materials available there. The villagers helped the visitors to prepare the food.

X

Swami Anandagiri and his disciples took a break in their trek and rested under a tree. They had no food the previous day. The sun was at zenith. Even though it was not hot at that height of the mountain, they were tired and hungry. A few feet away a stream of water was trickling down from a crevice between the rocks.

Sudhanva went to the water source and drank the clear water. However, the weakness due to lack of food could not be forced away. He returned and sat amongst his companions. He looked at his guru who sat his eyes closed. He leaned against the trunk of the tree to sit straight.

The disciples were critical of their guru. They were not happy at the insensitive attitude of guru towards their suffering. The guru did not speak a word. To Maruthi, he appeared as if he was waiting for somebody to bring food. He said the same to his companion Omkara, who was next to him, without the guru hearing him.

Then they heard some tired low voices. In a few moments, they saw three poorly clad young boys dragging their feet, heading towards them.

They went straight to the water stream as if they had not seen the mendicants there.

After drinking water they felt better. Now they noticed the guru and his followers. He opened his eyes just then with the sounds of the newcomers.

The three of them paid obeisance to the guru. They then begged humbly for food. The guru asked them as to who they were and why they were there.

One of them who was bold enough and appeared as leader said, "We had come from a village to escape the troubles inflicted on us by naxalites and police. We are going to the top of the mountain for seeking the grace of God for treasures. But now we are very tired and hungry. If you don't share food with us we will die. Kindly save us."

Sudhanva said they also faced the same problem.

The guru became emotional with his pity on them.

He asked his disciples to check whether anything was there in their bags to help the guests.

They in one voice replied that everything was exhausted the previous midday itself.

However the guru insisted them to check once again.

Each one of the disciples without any expectation had put their hands into the bags. Then a miracle happened. The disciples found to their surprise fruits of a number of varieties in their bags. They eagerly took them out. Sudhanva spread a cloth on the ground and all of them poured out the fruits on that. It became a big heap.

The guru asked the new comers to feast on them. After some time the guru and his companions too shared the fruits to appease their hunger.

The new comers did not know that there was nothing earlier in those bags.

The disciples thanked their guru by prostrating at his feet. The new-comers who were none other than Ramsaran and his friends, too followed suite. The guru said when it was necessary to save someone who had faith in Him, the Lord would not fail to come to rescue.

Ramsaran and friends however did not come to know about the miracle.

After resting for some time, they began their journey again.

Sudhanva asked the guru hesitantly to narrate any story to improve their knowledge of this world and the other.

The guru did not refuse.

He began "There was a king by name Surasena who ruled one of the states of the northern India in the days of yore. He was very prosperous. He had a number of wives but was not blessed with a child. He could not forget this lacuna and was worried ever.

One day a saint by name Angirasa came to the court of the king. The king pleased him with all the respects to be given to a saint. When enquired about the wellbeing of the king and his people, the king expressed his anguish for not being blessed with a child, though he did not lack anything else. The saint closed his eyes and was immersed in prayer. He appeared as if he sought the help of the Lord for removing the worry of the king.

After some time he opened eyes and asked the king to perform a Vedic-ritual for fulfilling his desire. The king made elaborate arrangements for performing the ritual. The saint himself supervised the performance of that ritual.

After completion of the ritual, the offerings remained would be taken as prasad. The prasad was given by the saint to the eldest queen to consume. Then he blessed the king and the eldest queen that they would get a son. But he also warned the elated king that same son would be the reason for his joy and sorrow in future.

Some months later the queen gave birth to a male child. The people of the entire kingdom celebrated the happy occasion. The king's joy had no barriers.

But there were other queens to the king who did not have children. They were neglected by the king. There were many bad people who wanted to take revenge on the king for some reason or other. They took advantage of the grouse of other queens and hatched a plot to kill the young prince.

One day when the mother of the boy, the first queen, was away, they poisoned his food and killed him.

The king and the queen had become personifications of sorrow.

At that time the saint Angirasa and the celestial singer Narada came to the king. And Angirasa began preaching him the philosophy of life.

He said, "Oh, king for whom you lament so much? This life is temporary. It is like a stream of water. It continuously flows. Like sand particles, we meet each other and separate again, may be to meet once more elsewhere. What is dying is the physical body which is made of five elements, but not the soul which is forever. The soul is a smaller part of the Supreme God and deathless. I came to you even in the first instance to teach you this only. But you were worried about children at that time. Now this calamity had occurred. You realize that this world is full of sorrow only. So now you work the rest of your life for reaching God."

Narada then said, "I will give you a divine mantra, which if you recite for a week you will obtain all great benefits."

But the king was not in a condition to listen and understand the wise words of Narada. So Narada tried another method. With his great powers, he brought back the soul which had left the body of the king's son, into this world again.

Addressing that soul which was in astral form, he appealed, "Oh blessed soul, look at the bereaved king and queen, your father and mother. Please take pity on them and enter the body again to please them. You can enjoy the stately pleasures."

The soul replied, "Oh saint Narada, I had many births and deaths till now. I also had many fathers and mothers. I took birth as a lowly creature of animal earlier and finally as human being. How can I satisfy these many parents? So I have no desire to enjoy royal treats either."

With those words the soul took leave of the great saints and disappeared.

The king heard all this conversation and realized the purpose of the life and death. He got rid of the snares of Maya and attained wisdom to seek the guidance of saints Angirasa and Narada."

The guru completed the story.

Ramsaran addressing the guru asked, "Sir, we used to watch dramas played in our village. They were generally about Ramayana and Mahabharata. I used to get some doubts about the stories."

The guru asked him to express them without any hesitation.

Ramsaran told him, "Swami, when I was watching the scene in which Droupadi was de-robed in Mahabharata, I felt that it was not befitting for a king to order such a heinous act to another royal personage, that too his own cousin's wife."

The guru replied, "When somebody is hurt so badly as Duryodhana by a woman, he may not be able distinguish the good from bad. His only intention would be to take revenge and that too in such a harsh way that he wanted to show everybody that he had an upper hand. You know that he was ill-treated in Maya-sabha palace by Droupadi in that story. She laughed at his travails while going around in that palace which was made with many illusory features. He was ill-treated in the presence of many other women."

Ramsaran again asked, "Sir, but even according to our country's great tradition it was against the common moral code to ill-treat a woman in the public. I am not convinced about the story that such a thing could happen in our great country."

The guru was not angry with him because he criticized the religious classic.

He smiled and said, "I wonder how deeply you thought about those incidents in the classic. I appreciate your respect for our traditions."

He further clarified, "The tradition was that ladies of royalty used to wear an upper cloth over the usual upper garment. That was not to be with menials. They had no upper cloth covering their bosom. So when the upper cloth of a lady of the royal family was removed, she was made equal to a servant. That was a great dishonor meted out to that lady. What was done to Droupadi was that."

Ramsaran smiled in satisfaction of a cleared doubt.

They reached a village by then.

The guru and his disciples enquired about the way to any temple, where they could stay for the night and proceeded thither. Ramsaran and friends left them after paying obeisance to the guru.

XI

Vacra was the first to wake up in his group. It was early in the morning. Many others were still sleeping. When he looked at his companions lying there on the ground in deep sleep, he felt the group was not as big as it was. First he thought it was because Manda was not there in the group. But he started counting now. Some of them had covered themselves in full, as was their habit. The number came to four only.

"Saral, get up, that is enough." He shouted in anxiety.

Saral woke up at once as he suspected something was amiss, as he heard his boss's anxious call.

Vacra asked him to check if everyone was there. The later saw each one's face, by pulling aside the bed sheets. He found two were missing.

He cried out nervously, "Boss, Shyama and Kali are not here."

The boss asked him to check if they had gone to attend nature's call.

With the high pitched conversation, others of their group woke up too.

Then, all of them began searching for the missing members. But the two missing persons could not be located.

They finished their ablutions, while guessing the reasons for the absence of their two colleagues. They were now five, including the boss. As it was a village, there was no possibility of the attack of a wild animal. Persons of other group who slept at a distance were busy with their chores.

There could be no mischief by them. In fact they only gave Vacra the medicine for snake bite. There was no reason to suspect them.

When Vacra and his group were anxiously discussing, it caught the eye of one of the other group. He came near Vacra and asked him the reason of their worry. Vacra looked at him sternly. But Saral explained him about their trouble. To that he reacted stating that he saw two of Vacra's group waking up early in the morning and walking away covered fully in bed sheets.

Vacra then could guess their intentions. At once he checked for his revolver in the bag. It was missing. The ammunition too was gone. So it was a planned action. They were bent on going to the mountain peak by themselves and grab as much as they can.

Vacra became very angry and he hit the stone slab on which he was sitting with his clenched fist so hard that the skin split and blood gushed out. He then went away towards the nearby trees. The informant from the other group was so scared that he left the scene at once.

After breakfast, whatever that could mean in those circumstances, Vacra and his four followers set off again on their journey. After a few moments the other group also was on the trek.

Vacra thought over the matter of lessening number in the group. He lost his revolver too. Now he was without an effective weapon. Knife was not suited to him, though he had one with him. He did not use knife much. That was for his followers. For using knife one should go closer to the opponent. It was risky. He felt that opponent should not be underestimated, before the first strike. Possessing a fire arm is different. Of course he was not afraid of opponents. But one should be cautious and also tactful in fights. It was of no use in being careless about safety.

A few days back he thought about elimination of his colleagues. But now without any action on his part, they became five from a group of eight. It was not clear to him if that was good for him or not. He thought however he needed some followers to support him, till he laid his hands on the treasures and also till he reached the base of the mountain back again. Elimination was not going to be difficult for him later. But these incidents are happening uncontrolled.

He made up his mind after much deliberation that he must add some new hands on the way by offering them some attractive benefits.

Then he recollected again about his lost revolver. Without that in his holster, he felt as if he lost one of his limbs. It was now impossible to acquire a revolver here on this mountain at any price. He must manage his men tactfully without that.

He looked back at his men. Saral and other three were walking with bent heads, each absorbed in his own thoughts. What were they thinking? With those unwanted incidents at the back of his mind, Vacra wished to know their thoughts, but how?

Vacra asked Saral, "Why did Shyama and Kali left us? Could you guess something?"

Saral was confused. As far as he guessed they were gone with the motive of gaining the entire treasure for themselves. Of course the other reason could be to get away from the dominance of the boss. But he could not tell that. His boss might be offended. Vacra was not a person to keep quite after getting offended. So it was risky to tell the truth to him.

Saral replied with a faded smile, "Boss, I could not guess any reason other than that they wanted to enjoy free trekking with a revolver in hand. They wanted some adventure, I think."

Vacra laughed away, pretending to take it easy on his erstwhile assistants.

"That's right, they wanted some adventure. It is not that easy to live an adventurous life. There is much risk—risk unknown and unexpected. They should not have done so."

Another of the followers ventured, "Boss, we may meet them again on the way. Will you accept them again?"

"Why not, they are our colleagues since many years. They wanted some adventure, okay, let them have it."

Vacra reflected—he wanted that only. He should meet them once more. They would know what price they would have to pay- to trick Vacra.

At a distance ahead of them, he saw silhouette figures of three men walking slowly as if they were very much tired.

Vacra cautioned his men to be on alert as they were now unarmed—in the sense they had no revolver. He asked Saral to lag behind them at a distance, so that if something happened he could be of help to them with an element of surprise played on the opponents.

They slowly approached the men going in front of them. After some time when they were close enough, they could make out that the three men in fact were young boys in their teens or twenty plus. Those three were very tired and were not in a condition to do Vacra and his men any harm.

Vacra asked the person who appeared to be the leader of them who they were and from where they came.

The leader who was none other than Ramsaran gave the information wanted by Vacra. He asked for some food.

Vacra readily asked his men to give them food and water. Ramsaran and his friends who were standing at a distance came forward. They appeased their hunger and sat down to rest under a tree there. Then Vacra talked to Ramsaran for some time to find out what kind of person he was.

Vacra was suspicious of Ramsaran though he wanted some men to add to his team. Ramsaran was knowledgeable and was not too submissive. But Vacra did not give away his reservations. He needed some support in his adventure. He thought he could exercise caution and study the newcomers, while allowing them to go with them.

Vacra and his men too had their food.

They were again on their trek, with Vacra in the lead.

XII

Shyama and Kali looked around them again and again, to make sure Vacra and his other men were not following them. He was not their boss any more. They need not care him. But they knew his cruel ways. He could be very dangerous even without his revolver. He was merciless with his adversaries.

By the time it was midday they were confident that Vacra and his dominance was history. Moreover, they had the revolver with them now, but not with the erstwhile boss.

They warbled and danced holding each other's hands with gay abandon. They walked fast without any exhaustion as they were on cloud nine.

After a while when they felt like eating, they rummaged through the bags and found rotis. Kali suggested they could now have some pleasure of hunting and eat the game for a change. They were armed with a revolver now.

As Kali was a better shot, he went around noiseless for some distance and at last shot a rabbit. He brought it back to where Shyama was resting.

Shyama made fun of the effort since with a fire arm Kali could have killed a deer but brought only a small rabbit. They cooked the meat and ate with rotis.

While they were enjoying thus, they were being watched by two persons with envy. They hid behind trees at a distance and waited for an opportunity to attack Kali and his friend by surprise.

Those two strangers were former constables of police, who were removed from service for their overzealous actions in dealing with the criminals. They killed away many criminals including some naxalites in encounters, without producing them in courts. They were hardcore killers. They were nick named Yamakinkaras, meaning servants of God of death.

Kali had kept the revolver close to his left hand while they were resting after the meal. Shyama was rolling from one side to the other. He could not sleep. He was lying to the left of Kali.

Y.K.-1 became impatient and he forced the other to follow him. They closed in on the resting duo from behind the trees, without making noise.

When they were very close to the two erstwhile Vacra's assistants, they jumped on them. As Kali was sleeping he became a victim to the knife of one of the Y.K.s.

Shyama's right hand was close to the left hand of Kali and next to that was the revolver.

Shyama sat erect at once with the revolver in hand. He fired it without proper aim. He was not a good shot any time. But the bullet hit Y.K.-2 in the right upper arm and he became ineffective. He pressed the wound with the handkerchief and tied it around the arm to stop the blood.

Y.K.-1 now jumped on Shyama and snatched away the firearm. He then plunged a knife into the stomach of Shyama. Next he made sure that Kali would not get up and stabbed him again with the knife on his back as he was lying face down on the ground. Both the victims became motionless and lied in pools of blood sinking in the ground.

The Y.K.s then ransacked the belongings of the victims and collected all useful things. They then walked away, after Y.K.-2 got a cloth bandage fixed to his right arm over the wound.

Y.K.-2 felt giddy with the loss of blood from the wound. They stopped under a tree close by.

Y.K.-1 said, "Friend, we will have food now. You will gain some energy to resume the journey."

He unpacked the bags snatched away from their victims a short while ago. There were food materials sufficient for two for a couple of days in them.

After eating food Y.K.-2 said with a smile, "Now I am all right. Whenever you want, we will start again."

Y.K.-1 said, "Not so fast, my friend. The bullet is in there. That has to be removed. You must have first-aid for the wound you know. It should not become septic."

He made a fire with the dry twigs picked around. He pulled out the bottle of brandy from his bag and gave it to Y.K.-2. He burnt the knife in the fire.

Meanwhile Y.K.-2 had two long swigs at the brandy bottle.

Y.K.-1 opened the bandage on the right arm of Y.K.-2. He asked Y.K.-2 to turn his gaze aside and thrust the knife into the wound and pulled the bullet out within seconds. He used cloth pieces to stop the bleeding. He then made a cloth piece wet with the brandy and pressed it against the wound. Y.K.-2 gave a piercing cry of severe pain.

Y.K.-1 made a fresh bandage on the other's arm.

They rested for a long time till Y.K.-2 was ready. They started on the trek again.

* * *

Vacra in the lead and with stomachs full with food, the visitors made a fast trek among the forest of short trees and bushes. Vacra suddenly thought he heard the voice of Shyama at a distance.

He asked Saral, "Did you hear voice of someone suffering in pain?"

"No boss, I have not heard any such thing."

Saral looked at his companion Grahi in disbelief. He smiled with understanding. They were of the opinion that Vacra was imagining things. What could that be? Was he losing his balance?

Saral ventured, "Boss, please forget about those ungrateful fellows."

Vacra looked at Saral sternly and said, "I am not mad. I heard that. It was certainly the voice of Shyama."

After passing some distance they all heard those low wails.

Presently they saw Shyama and Kali lying in pools of blood. Shyama was still with life and groaning with pain. Kali was motionless.

Vacra rushed forward and held the head of Shyama in his hands. He asked for water from his companions and poured water into the mouth of Shyama, who drank it with difficulty. He opened his eyes and stunned with fear for a moment and then he smiled.

Vacra too smiled to give him confidence. Shyama appeared suffering severely.

Vacra's other followers wondered as to how their boss could become so docile to forget the treachery of the men who abandoned him.

Vacra asked Shyama, "You forget about what you did to me. I forgive you. But let me know what happened to you? Who did this to you?"

Shyama with half opened eyes and in low voice replied, "Boss two wretches suddenly pounced on us and injured severely. Kali died and I am alive as of now. Pardon me."

Vacra asked "Where are they? Who could they be?"

Shyama in a very feeble voice replied, "They appeared to be former police men. They went ahead on this way."

He pointed out the direction with his right hand limply and then closed his eyes. He was like a burnt away candle, almost burnt.

Vacra then remembered about his revolver.

He asked, "Shyama, where is the revolver?"

Shyama half opened his eyes and replied "They took that away."

Then he again closed his eyes never to open again. He was dead.

In the mean while Saral checked for the pulse of Kali. He was no more.

Vacra now cursed his dead followers, for their foolish adventure. His men then dug deep trenches to bury the bodies. With heavy hearts and sorrow they left the place.

Vacra said to his followers, "Now we have to be watchful about those killers. They appear to be ruthless. They are ahead of us on this way. If necessary we may have to kill them to save ourselves."

All of them were of the same opinion on that. They were scared of those thugs after seeing the way their colleagues were killed.

Vacra said they must be ready all time with their weapons, whatever weapons they had. They had knives good enough to kill a person with one hard stroke. They were not new at using weapons. They knew that even Shyama and Kali must have been taken unaware of for suffering those injuries. Those two were not softies to take the stabbings lying low on the ground.

They, Vacra and his burglar colleagues followed by Ramsaran and his friends walked forward watching surroundings with care.

There was some sudden movement in the bushes on the left side. Everybody became alert and ready to hit. A rabbit ran away from one side to the other escaping them.

Saral laughed loudly. All others found it hilarious too.

But unexpectedly two strangers in pants and shirts, from the bushes rushed towards the side where Vacra was. One of them pierced Grahi with his knife. The second fellow fired at Vacra with a revolver, who was pushed aside in time by Ramsaran. The bullet grazed the skin of the latter's left hand. Within no time Vacra made a cut at the throat of that man with his long knife. His throat was half cut and he fell bleeding. The moment the revolver fell down from his hand, Vacra took it. He kissed it with affection as if it were a child reunited after a long time.

In the mean time the first fellow who was none other than Y.K.-1 pounced on Ramsaran and tried to kill him with his knife. Ramsaran tried to escape, however his right cheek was cut.

Within seconds after that Vacra who was ready with his revolver again, shot at Y.K.-1 at the chest and killed him instantaneously.

Vacra searched for the ammunition of the revolver in the baggage of Y.K.-2 and took away all needed things along with the ammunition from that baggage.

Grahi was seriously injured. He was pierced in the lower part of the abdomen. Two others were injured too. Ramsaran used some wild leaves available there to stop bleeding on his cheek and injuries of others too. He and Saral attended to Grahi who could be on his feet again after some rest. Ramsaran and Saral helped him in walking slowly.

They were in the midst of the forest infested with wild animals. They heard sounds of movement of those in the bushes around. The smell of fresh blood and flesh close by was inviting to them.

When checked they found Y.K.-1 and Y.K.-2 were dead by then.

It was becoming dark and there was not much time left for them to secure the safe haven of some village. They were of one opinion in abandoning the bodies of the cruel attackers in the forest as they were. There was no time for digging trenches and burying them. So they left those two bodies there and made haste towards the village expected to be close by.

XIII

Charudas resumed his story telling.

"I will relate another interesting story. Long time back, that was in the days of kings and kingdoms, a young man by name Sunder lived with his beautiful wife. He was a weaver by profession. He used to make saris and other dress materials on order. His wife and parents used to help him in his work. As he was a good designer, unlike other weavers he never had any problem in selling his wares. People used to come, discuss and give orders for the materials required for marriages and functions.

But this young man Sunder was a man of many desires. He used to daydream about the women who came to him on business. He used to be jealous of their husbands. His friend Dharam advised him many times against such tendencies on his part.

During the course of his talk with friends he came to know about a woman whose husband was a cuckold. When that woman came to him on business, he made more than required acquaintance with her. She was a rich woman. She studied him for a few months. When she felt that there would not be any harm from him, she accepted him.

He became bolder now and his behavior with other woman customers of young age became questionable. During the course of his business he used to visit the houses of the customers for clarifications on design or for collection of dues from them some times. On one such occasion, he misbehaved with a woman, and got severe scolding from that family. This was slowly spreading among the people of the place.

One of his distant relatives, Jagan who did not like the success of Sunder in business, took this bad news about him as an advantage. As he was a junior employee in the court of the king, he informed about the bad behavior of Sunder to his boss. Incidentally he also told about the beauty and grace of the wife of Sunder. He exaggerated those qualities while narrating to attract the attention of the king's courtiers, intending thereby some harm or other to Sunder's wife.

As expected by Jagan, one of the king's courtiers Krupa, who was bad enough to take advantage of people's weaknesses sent his men one night in the disguise of thieves and ordered Sunder's wife to be brought to his palace. They beat Sunder and carried his wife away.

Luckily for Sunder, the king was on his monthly surprise visit to the town. His soldiers stopped the thieves and the wife of Sunder was restored to him. Krupa was punished for the crime.

With this incident Sunder was shocked to know what it was to lose one's wife to others. He became a good man thenceforth."

Charudas stopped the story and looked around. The listeners were not bored, he was sure.

He asked not addressing anybody in particular, "Is this interesting?"

Veera replied "Sir, you wrote this story by imagination or did you come across anybody of that nature?"

Charudas "When I write a story it need not reflect any real incidents. I think nobody likes that. Many characters are imaginary. Even if some look like existing ones it might be accidental and unexpected. Sometimes if a writer is influenced by someone he might include that character or a modified version of that in the writing unintentionally. Other times the writer may like to tell something for social good. He imagines the incidents and characters for bringing out the effect of that notion."

Nishit asked Charudas to narrate another one. All eyes were riveted on the writer.

Veera felt something was amiss at that time. He did not find his wife Chandra beside him.

After a few moments he saw her coming towards him from behind a tree. He also saw Sharad walking slowly at a distance to the place where they were sitting.

Veera told her not to go alone as it was not safe in those parts. She replied she did not go alone and she was safe.

Veera looked around if anybody was watching them. But nobody appeared to be aware of their conversation. It was real unawareness or intended unobtrusiveness, he could not make out.

Charudas resumed with a beaming face, "The story now I am going to narrate is about the dangers of action without prior thinking. That happens when one is arrogant and over confident or when he acts in anger.

Nishit said with a smile, "So you are going to tell us a moral story."

"Even the one we have heard must be a moral teaching," Sharad said.

Veera controlling anger, "But you did not listen that story, I think."

He knew the other's overtures towards his wife.

Sharad did not reply.

Charudas began "In the city of Mumbai—these incidents happened in and around the city—in one township, there lived a man named Arya. He belonged to a middle class family. He worked in an office as a supervisor of a section. His boss was a cunning man. He used to get work done without any extra expenditure to the office. He used to treat the staff well but never paid any wages for the overtime work. But when somebody was late he used to take the supervisor to task. The supervisor had to take action against his staff. Thus the supervisor used to act as a buffer between the boss and the staff. All the blame for action taken against the staff used to be left with supervisor. The boss managed to keep up his image of a good and efficient man in this manner. The supervisors knew the tricks played by the boss. But they could not do anything. The boss used to boast in official circles that he implemented good management practices in his office.

Sometimes the worries of office percolate to the homes of the individuals. This is more so when that person is egoistic or if he could not absorb the pressure within himself.

In the case of Arya this proved to take a toll on his family life.

One evening when he came late from office, his one year old son was crying in a very high pitch. His mother was trying to pacify the boy. That day Arya had a show down with his boss in the office. The work allotted to him could not be finished in time. Two of his assistants were absent that day. He was blamed even for this absence. Arya himself had to do the primary work of his assistants. Added to that, the tantrums of his boss made him mad. It told on his patience. He gave his piece of mind to his boss.

Back home, he tried to console the boy for some time. It did not help. He then shouted at the boy. The boy increased the pitch. Arya was drinking coffee. In a fit of rage, he threw the cup of coffee at the boy. Luckily for him and the boy, only some part of the coffee fell on him. With pain inflicted on him, the boy cried still high and soon fell unconscious. His mother threw cold water on the burnt place as well as on the face of the boy. Within a few moments he regained consciousness.

Arya felt bad for his short temper. His wife kept quiet. She knew no purpose would be served by trying to reason with him. He was adamant and vain glorious in mentality.

Arya could not bear the painful incident, the damage caused by his uncontrolled anger and the result of the misdeed. He walked out of the house.

He returned late in the night. Again his wife too suffered. One misdeed led to another. He did not eat till then. His wife was punished for the same reason. How could she eat without him? She knew he suffered by blaming himself for the incident of the morning and repenting the same all the time. She also knew he was beyond him in doing the same.

She was a clear headed woman. They were reconciled on the bed at last.

It was a nice early winter morning. The morning sun was pleasant. The surroundings appeared as if painted in light orange color. The elderly and those who needed exercise were coming out of houses for morning walk with smiling faces. They greeted each other. Arya's neighbor Raghu greeted him, wishing him a very good morning.

It took time for Arya to come to grips with the pleasant ambience of the morning. He however belatedly returned the gesture.

Arya was engrossed in the memories of previous day's arguments with his boss. Finally when he was on his way home, he remembered that boss had asked him to finalize the file on hand by noon of next day. It involved much work. He could not work the previous night with the unwanted incident of that day. He became nervous now. He was ready to go to office.

It was nine o'clock. But the clock in the hall was slow by ten minutes. His wife forgot that and she did not keep his lunch box ready. He was waiting in the verandah. At last when she came and handed the box, he was angry. With that anger he started the scooter and lost control. It dashed on to the road opposite with speed and hit a cycle born man. In turn that person fell on a motor bike man. The combined effect was one broken bone to him and many injuries to others. He was to be lifted back inside by the onlookers. With the intervention of the neighbors the police relented. But he had to pay heavy compensation to all involved.

Later his distant cousin who visited him asked him to go to a Baba of the next village for some talisman to get rid of the ill-luck.

Promptly they visited that Baba. The Baba checked his horoscope and lines on his palm. He advised Arya to be patient with the work and the world. He gave him a talisman which was to be tied to his left upper arm. He asked him to touch that and think of him, whenever he was in trouble. He warned him not to do anything before that.

It appeared that the talisman worked. Arya did nothing thereafter, without following the Baba's instructions. He was not in trouble again and his wife was happy."

Charudas stopped the narration.

Nishit was surprised to hear that.

"Sir, how could that simple instruction of the Baba and talisman solved his ego problem. That was a psychic problem too," Nishit expressed his doubt.

"The solution did not lie in the talisman or Baba. It was the wise instruction—to wait to touch the talisman and think of the Baba—that cured him. During that short period his anger could be subsided due to the diversion of his mind to a different subject. Arya's anger was sudden and was for a short period. The Baba knew that and he gave him that wise advice," said Charudas.

XIV

Vacra was a wiser man now. With all these pleasant and not so pleasant experiences he knew it was no good to be harsh with the people he came across. It was not like his previous vocation where his word was law to his followers and also to his victims. He avoided being trigger happy. He remembered the good act of Ramsaran in saving him.

They now reached the village they expected to reach a short while ago.

They had a wash with the water available in the large well beside the ashram. Only Grahi was not seen near the well. He could not rise from his bed. He suffered with high fever.

The visitors were fed well at the ashram. There was a chest to collect donations in cash or kind. Some had put cash and others eatables into the chest. Some others paid in golden ornaments. They might be thinking of the treasures they were going to get later and were ready to lose those small things they had, for common good. Some others those in the group of Vacra did not lose sight of that and were scheming to acquire them. Later when they were alone, Vacra warned them against that. He was reformed to that extent now. He did not want to be delayed or restrained in his trek by the consequences of those small time attractions. New terrain and new kind of people, these villagers could not be taken for granted.

Now they found that Grahi was not in those who ate and rested. He did not get up. When Saral checked for his pulse, he was no more.

With heavy hearts they cremated his body there in that village, after collecting some mementos of his personal belongings to be handed over to his family members later.

After breakfast next day, they got lunch packed and were ready to start again. Vacra's followers were not happy and enthusiastic as before. The death of four of their colleagues in all, snatched away the pleasure of the tedious though interesting trek. Ramsaran and his two companions stood behind Vacra ready to follow them.

Just at that time the group of Charudas and others reached the ashram. They appeared very tired.

Ramsaran greeted Charudas.

Charudas was surprised and pleased to meet him again.

"We were held up at the previous place. In fact it was my mistake to go on narrating stories, to these people. After that we could not reach any village by night. We spent the night without sleep in the open over those rocks, a very bitter experience," he said.

"What about your food, sir?" Ramsaran queried in good nature.

Vacra did not like the familiarity between those two people. He wanted to groom Ramsaran as one amongst them. But now he knew he had many other friends among the visitors to the mountain.

"We had something in bags. We had to satisfy with that. Are you now ready to go?" Charudas asked him.

Ramsaran thought over quickly. He saw Vacra and his associates at close quarters during their previous trek. He did not know their activities prior to coming on this trip. But their mannerisms, people they had confronted on the way and their ways of dealing with them created an adverse impression on him. He decided to follow Charudas group for obvious reasons. He looked at Vacra, who was eying him not so pleasantly.

However, Ramsaran did not mind that. He came a long way to care such threats and fears.

He told Vacra, "Sir, I come later."

Vacra did not answer and walked away, his men following in the rear.

Once on the trek he said, "I had seen many such fellows. I thought he would fit in our group. But that was not to be. He is not reliable."

His men were not eager to respond.

He wanted to cheer them up.

"I will narrate a short incident to show how good I was in my boyhood. I had to mould myself tough later due to many troublesome incidents in my life.

I was prepared for deceptions such as these, I mean that fellow Ramsaran.

Now to the interesting incident—I was ten years old then. I was traveling with my uncle to my grandparent's place.

We were at the railway station, waiting for the train. The bench on which we sat, it was a cement bench, had some hollow place under one of its legs. A large cockroach slowly came out of that. I was afraid to see such a big cockroach. My uncle made fun of me for that.

The creature slowly moved towards the edge of the platform, down which there were rail lines. With the sounds of moving passengers it returned to the hiding place. I went to see what is that, that attracted it beyond the edge of the platform. It was all full of filth, banana peels, and leftovers of food packets and so on. So that was what attracted it, I thought. It must be the food available to it readily. It had the smell of it, probably.

It happened so, a number of times. I was afraid that it might be crushed under the feet of some passenger in a hurry. I tried to bring to the notice of the passengers who were likely to pass that way, about the insect. They used to laugh and go away. I was happy to have saved its life. My uncle too was observing me and smiled at my antics to scare that insect away a number times, to save it from the shoes of many passengers.

At last after a long wait our train was announced. It treaded on to the platform slowly. The passengers hurried to enter the compartment of their allotment.

My uncle pulled at my hand to follow him fast. We took our bags in hand and ran towards our compartment.

At that moment, I felt that something was crushed under my feet and a feeble sound to that effect reached my ear. It was none other than the cockroach which I was trying to save from others feet. I suffered a feeling of helplessness, pity and remorse for that unintended harm I caused to that creature.

Since then, I learnt a lesson not to be too concerned for things, I was not responsible for and not to assume responsibility for things beyond my capability."

Now Vacra looked at his men three in all, Saral included. Saral is the only reliable person among them and was with him since many years. He felt sad for the situation. He started with seven men and now left with three. Those two who abandoned him had a good lesson. He did not want to remember their names even. They suffered for the deception they played on him. But is it alright with three men as followers?

He thought over for some time. But as he thought earlier, company of more men was not merrier any more. Each man was a share, a loss in the treasure. Moreover he did not need any supporters in this terrain. It was an individual effort. It was not group work, as in his previous vocation. Someone to come to rescue in times of necessity was welcome, however. That was why he thought of including Ramsaran and his fellows in his group. But that was not to be. He was not reliable and would not stick to one group. He had many friends.

"Boss, we can stop under that tree for lunch." Saral suggested to him.

Vacra's mind reverted to the present.

He assented.

They finished their lunch. The weather was good. There was no drizzle, the usual phenomenon, on those hills at that height. They rested under the tree. Vacra thought of the progress they made. It was told that they had passed the third camp. That was long time back. That was before the death of Manda.

He talked aloud as if to himself, "I don't know where we are now?"

Saral too was thinking about that.

He said "We passed camp three, boss. Later we were besieged with the calamities one after another. There was no opportunity to think about the progress we made."

"We have to find out our present position, when we meet somebody in the next village. But I think we are on right track as we are meeting many visitors on this path." Vacra said

"But boss, are we following the shortest route?"

"But we had bitter experiences when we followed shorter or safer routes. We lost our colleagues and met with many accidents. So it is better now to seek and accept some people for company."

They rested for a long time, as they were tired. They awoke with the low sounds of repeated uttering of 'Om'. The sound emanated from a short distance.

"Some ascetic is praying in this jungle. He must be a true saint, to have come this far and spending his time praying instead of going for treasures," said Vacra.

He got to his feet and asked others to follow him. Avoiding the long ant-lines, the ants were large too, on the ground and in the midst of the heaps of dead leaves they walked along an un-trodden path.

After some time, they reached the place from where the sound was coming forth. The person who was praying or meditating as they say, was seated on an elevated rock.

"Swami! Swami!" Vacra called aloud to catch the attention of that saint. But that person was engrossed in deep prayer and was not moving.

Vacra's desire to seek an easy advantage or a blessing or boon from that ascetic strengthened now. It was clear that he was not an ordinary mendicant, his attentive prayer proved that. Vacra thought he could ask for some mantra or talisman to have some permanent benefit. He would not regret then, this trip to the mountain, result of which he was not sure of yet.

He again ventured to call out. In the meantime his followers too tried to help their boss.

In this melee they did not notice the arrival of the group of Charudas there. They came to that spot hearing the shouts of Vacra and his men. In fact they were going on the footpath which visitors use. They diverted to this route to meet and warn Vacra and his men.

Charudas went near Vacra and touched him on the shoulder to get his attention. Then he called him aside. He explained that it was not right to disturb the saint from his prayer. He might become a victim to the anger of the latter, whether the saint desired it or not; the anger of such saints was so potent. So it was better to wait till he comes out of meditation, to talk to him. An unwilling Vacra came away from that spot at last.

It was getting dark. So on much persuasion by Charudas, he abandoned the desire to talk to the saint and walked along with others to the nearest village.

* * *

Charudas was persuaded by his group of companions to continue with his stories, after the night meal.

The narrator leaned back against the clay wall of the ashram. It was not comfortable however. There were small pebbles sticking out of the wall, which were hurting him. He covered his back with a towel.

Vacra in the meantime, wanted to clear his doubt about the location of the place where they were. He wanted to know how far he was away from the treasure.

He asked Charudas about that. Charudas replied that as far as he knew, they had passed the third camp and they must be close to the fourth or they might as well be in fourth one.

He called one of the men of the ashram and asked about his doubt.

"Sir, we are not aware of that terminology of camps and so on," the other man replied.

“All right then. Please tell me in how many days we can reach the top of the mountain from here?”

“We could go to the place near that in three days. But for you it takes more time. You know we are accustomed to this terrain.”

“But why have you not gone to the top place? Are you not interested in treasures?”

“Sir, we know we will not get an undeserved boon. So we prepare ourselves for becoming worthy of that.”

“In that case how about us?”

“That depends on one’s merits. You have to assess yourself.”

Those who listened to the conversation wondered how a layman like him, who they took to be a worker in the ashram, could answer the queries of Charudas so convincingly. He appeared uninformed and very ordinary. But his answers gave away his depth of knowledge.

Vacra was however happy to know that they were as close as three days to the treasures. He then thought of the shares he had to forego. He counted the total number of persons assembled there. Charudas and his group were a dozen or so, Ramsaran and his two friends, then himself and his three men—in total about a score of aspirants. He wanted to count in terms of approximation because nobody could be sure of eventual arrival at the top. Taking his own case, he started with seven and now left with three only.

He continued to assess—out of these twenty how many will reach the sixth camp.

In the meantime, Charudas began his story.

He said “My friends, I told you about the disasters of two out of the six characteristics to be desisted.

The next enemy within is miserliness."

He looked around as some of them were talking amongst themselves. It was about reaching of the final camp. They had become enthusiastic with the information that they were to reach that in three days.

Charudas corrected them, "It might be three days for these people but not for us."

But they were not inclined to accept that. After all these days of intense effort and after coming to know how close they were to the final camp, it was difficult to admit their inability. They started to imagine things about the treasures.

Vacra was considering all of them, except his three men as enemies.

Charudas began again, "Friends, forget about the treasures for the time being. We are still away from them, may be five days or even a week. We need not bother about that now. Having come this far, we will not be deprived of them I think."

Sudhama laughed loudly and said, "I agree with him. We should not be excited about the treasures. It is also advisable to keep ourselves peaceful, so that there would not be any animosity amongst us."

There was calmness now amongst them. They pondered over that advice and asked Charudas to continue in one voice.

Charudas smiled "Now you listen to the story and enjoy. These stories are written to entertain the reader. That was the first consideration. If somebody thought that there was some principle worth emulating, that's up to him to consider.

On the shores of river Narmada, long ago there used to live one merchant by name, Lobha Gupta in a town under the rule of a king by name Marthanda Verma. Lobha Gupta was very greedy in his dealings with his customers. People used to hate him and his methods but as he was a rich man and versatility of his wares, his name was the last word in business. He earned much and used to keep all his riches in gold and diamonds only. He was averse to keep immovable properties. His logic was that he could readily shift to another important city when the business becomes dull in the present place. Another advantage for him was that the king and his officials could not assess all his wealth for tax purposes. He could avoid paying tax. He kept two sturdy watchmen armed well to protect his family and wealth.

Attempts were made by thieves to loot that merchant many times, but they could not succeed. He kept some important officials of the kingdom in good humor, so that they would be of use in case of necessity. He considered spending on them as good investment for his business.

During the days of calamities he used to reap the advantage by hoarding the daily needed commodities in advance and selling them at high prices when the demand was high.

During one monsoon, river Narmada was in floods.

Lobha Gupta was benefited by selling the food grains at high prices. People were in distress. They approached the king for succor.

Differences arose between the king's officials and Gupta over the amounts payable to the former. Gupta was not yielding to pay anything more than the usual fixed sum to them.

Those officials carried complaints against the merchant to the king. The king sent his men to check his godowns. They found the hoarded merchandise and transferred it to the king's granary for distribution to the needy. The merchant became worried. It never happened to him before. He did not expect the officials to be ruthless towards him, who had been paying them so long.

Later on his position became worse. The king was angry with him. Even the officials became enemies to him now.

So as planned by him in advance, he converted all the remaining money into gold. Then one night, as prearranged by him, he collected his gold and valuables and started with his family of wife and a son, on bullock carts.

He was to cross river Narmada to reach the city of his destination. He shifted all his belongings to a hired boat and continued his further journey with his family.

After going for some time, the boat developed a hole in the bottom. Water slowly entered in. The merchant and his family were scared. The boat man handled the oars. So he asked the merchant to remove the water in the boat with help of a pitcher kept in the boat. But as the boat advanced into the river further, the water gushing into the boat became more. At one stage, the boat man asked the merchant to lessen his belongings so that their lives could be saved. He did not know that they were valuables and gold. But it was a necessity to lessen the weight, whether they were valuables or otherwise. The merchant was not inclined to lose his hard earned wealth. So the boat was slowly going down into the waters. The boat man advised the latter again to save his family of wife and son and throw away other belongings in the water. The merchant did not relent. The boatman then jumped into the river and went away swimming to his safety.

The merchant's wife wailed and asked him to throw the wealth for the sake of their son. The merchant clung to his wealth. His son was then washed away with a heavy current. His wife went after her son into the water. But even that could not save the merchant and his wealth. He was drowned along with his gold and diamonds in the water.

The miserly man could neither save his family and himself nor the wealth. He lost everything with his foolish attachment to the wealth."

Charudas halted to have a deep breath and some water to soak his throat.

* * *

Sudhama accompanied by Nishit walked towards back side of the ashram. On the way beside a tree two persons were in conversation in dark. They could only discern the silhouette forms. By their voices Nishit could identify them as Chandra, wife of Veera and the other as Sharad.

Sudhama said in low voice, "This is another case of treachery as that you suffered."

Nishit nodded in agreement.

After walking further, Nishit saw a number of flat stones over a ground well cleaned. Some people were sitting on those stones in meditation.

Sudhama directed Nishit to some secluded spot there and they occupied two stone seats. He then guided Nishit in meditation.

* * *

Charudas began another story.

"In a town called Nagoor, there lived a rich landlord Dhanaraj. He had so much of landed property and gold and precious stones that would be sufficient for a few generations even if they don't work for an earning. He had a son by name Kuberkumar.

He was given the best available education in those times by his father. After finishing his studies, he began taking part in the administration of his properties. His father was happy with the work of his son.

Dhanaraj then thought of marrying his son to a girl from a good family. He began looking for a suitable girl for him.

But his son had a girlfriend during his studies in another town. He loved her. The girl too loved him much. He did not forget her, though he was away from that place. He was however afraid to reveal this to his father.

It was not customary in their family to ask the consent of the boy before fixing the marriage. So his marriage was fixed with the daughter of a rich businessman. The marriage was performed grandly and the couple lived happily for some time.

After some days, on the pretext of business tour, Kuberkumar went to the place where his lover lived. He met her parents. He told them about his love for their daughter and that his parents could not come there to talk to them about the proposal. He presented them costly gifts.

The parents of the girl initially doubted his words. However, they were convinced about his sincere love later. They thought if he was not sincere in his love he would not have come that far for the sake of an ordinary girl. He appeared rich and belonged to a good family. The girl too liked him.

They married their daughter to him. After a few days Kuberkumar left his second wife and returned to his first wife. He gave some suitable reason for the delay in returning to his place.

He used to live with the two wives thus for some time.

Once during his tours, his father came to know about his son's second marriage through some business contacts. He was taking lunch at that time with other businessmen. He was very much hurt for the way his pampered son treated him. The pain caused him a heart attack. He died then and there. That place was none other than the town where his second daughter in law lived.

Kuberkumar's second father in law helped him to take his body back to his native place. Thus he came to know that his son in law was already married earlier.

Kuberkumar has become a free man now. Till then he was afraid of his father about his second marriage. He began spending more time at the second wife's house. He had built a mansion for her at her place. His first wife came to know of his second marriage.

His first wife did not have any children. The second one gave birth to a beautiful baby girl. He celebrated the occasion grandly. As he spent most of his time at the house of the second wife, his business began yielding lesser and lesser profits. He was fond of his daughter very much.

Later, his second wife became bed ridden with some incurable decease. She died after six months. She died however with the satisfaction that her husband looks after the baby so well.

Kuberkumar had a brother in law who looked after the business during his absence from the city. He was brother of his first wife. Together, the brother and sister managed to transfer away properties and business to their own benefit. Though Kuberkumar got information about the mischief of his wife and brother in law, he did not take proper action in time. So in course of time, he lost all his properties except for the mansion at the place of his second wife.

His daughter came of age. He could not provide her very best education as was given to him by his father. He felt bad for his inability.

Later he came to know that she loved her class mate who was the son of a teacher of her class. He asked her to desist from meeting him. But she said she would only marry him and none else. Perforce he married her to that boy, who was a small time businessman.

With all these adversities, Kuberkumar could not survive long. He died a disappointed man."

Charudas took a long breath to indicate the end of the story.

Somebody in the assembled yawned loudly, indicating their desire to end the session.

Charudas thanked his audience for the patience they showed to him.

Next day early in the morning, they woke up with the loud shrieks of Veera complaining about the absence of his wife who slept beside him the previous night.

Charudas asked Ramsaran to look for her in the surrounding places. He went with his friends and after some time returned without any clues to the absence.

Veera was wailing pitiably. He too went hither thither, and searched for her. Nishit took him aside beyond the hearing range of others and told him what he saw the previous night. Veera said he knew about her weakness but did not expect her to abandon him so fast. Sudhama came to him and consoled him.

XV

Vacra and his men went to the outskirts of the village for morning ablutions. After finishing the work, they were returning when they saw Ramsaran accompanied by his friends at a distance. Vacra wanted to tease them, as he was angry with him for not accompanying him on the previous occasion. He aimed his revolver at a bird on the tree near them. He shot the bird and it fell just a few feet away in front of Ramsaran. Ramsaran and friends were stunned at the sound. His friends gave a loud cry with fear.

Vacra laughed loudly at their plight. Ramsaran kept his cool.

Saral went and picked up the game. They all moved on towards the village.

For breakfast they had wheat gruel. Nothing else was available there. After breakfast many of the visitors were reluctant to start on the trek again. They felt that place very good for relaxing and one day's relaxation after so much trekking, appeared very much desirable. It was like a hard earned holiday after a weekday's work. Moreover the final destination was only three days away. With that line of thinking, by consensus they decided to rest at that place for one day.

After breakfast, there was group singing conducted by a swami attached to the ashram. This was different from other ashrams they saw on the way. There were no religious ceremonies attached to the ashrams. The ashrams there were only for the benefit of the visitors for their food and rest.

After singing session those desired went into the yard for meditation. Veera now joined Nishit in that exercise under the guidance of Sudhama.

The people who maintained the ashram, called the group of pilgrims for lunch. The lunch was a simple one with two dishes.

After lunch, a reluctant Charudas was persuaded by the group to narrate some more of the stories written by him for spending time.

They all proceeded to the place where meditation takes place twice a day in the morning and evening.

Charudas began, "Now this is about the disaster one suffers for possessing vanity beyond limits. There was once a king named Yasasakta ruling most of the northern parts of the land. He was a man of great valor and political scheming. He used to take advantage of the squabbles among the smaller kingdoms near his land. He used to take the side of the weaker of the two and help him win the other one. Thus he got the loyalty of the victorious one and the victorious king got the land of the vanquished.

When the kingdoms around his land were powerful, he used to sow seeds of difference between one king and his neighboring one. Thereafter he sends messages of offering help to the weaker one and wins his loyalty.

He was more feared than respected by his people by his arrogant behavior and ways of rule of law.

He depended more on the informants about the state of the affairs of the land. If the informant was biased, which happens more often than not, the people were to lose.

The king was very arrogant and he did not take any disrespect to him or to his rule of law lightly. The punishments were severe. The penalties were heavy. The coffers of the king grew bulky by the day. He was known to be a very rich king.

Instances of his excess arrogance were repeatedly talked about, in close circles of the people.

It was said that he did not like even his shadow on the ground to be trampled upon though unintentionally by anybody.

One day the king and his minister were on their way to the king's court. The minister to save his coat from getting wet in a water pool on his way stepped by mistake on the shadow of the king made by the morning sun. The king pushed him aside so forcefully, that the minister fell forward on the ground. A few footmen and bearers, who were there, watched this happening. By the time the king and minister reached the court hall, those who witnessed that incident lost their lives. Even though it was exaggerated people liked to believe the cruel deeds of their king as they lost loyalty to him.

The king ruled thus for some years. His only son, Yasassikhara, the prince, inculcated the qualities of his father in letter and spirit. He too was vainglorious and greedy and often corrupt in revenue collection.

The king was not in the know of these things. Anybody if dared to carry such information to the king would be dead the next moment. People knew that and behaved according to the dictates of the prince.

As he grew into a young man, the prince began developing a parallel work force for his purposes. In fact, they were armed gangs trained to suit his purposes. He used them even for other than his normal duties. He got his youthful fancies fulfilled with the help of these men.

The king came to know of these nefarious activities of the prince, in due course of time. He thought if such crimes against the people continued, his kingdom would not last long. He knew other kings around his land were watching to get even with him. They might avenge him and pay him in the same coin as was done earlier by him.

Yasasakta sent word for the prince. The prince was surprised at this. His father never called him to his official chambers. The king asked his son to take seat. After usual informal talk, he enquired about his nefarious activities. The prince did not come forward with the truth and he denied the allegations. The king became angry and warned him of consequences of such activities in the long run. Even though the king talked to him as a well wisher, the prince was shocked coming to know his limits, of which he was not aware of till then. The shock turned into shame. He felt ashamed in front of his father for the first time. The shame and his inability to retaliate turned into anger. He walked away from his presence angrily.

The king became a worried man since then. He tried to make his son turn a new leaf, by asking some wise men to advise him. Not many dared to pick enmity with the prince by advising him.

After some days, the king, on the advice of his minister, persuaded Charuhasa the courteson girl whom the prince adored much, to help change his ways. The prince refused her advices and in turn he elicited the information that the king only was responsible for her unusual attempt.

The king then decided to force his son to change by reducing his powers. He was asked not to be involved in the collection of taxes. The prince took that as an affront to his dignity.

Yasassikhara, the prince then began plotting with his friends and advisers to get back his powers. He discussed the methods available for that. Finally it boiled down to the fact that the king would not retrace his action by normal ways. That means he was to be forced into that action.

The prince waited for his opportunity.

The people of the kingdom celebrate every year, the day of king's ascension to the throne. On that day the king would be in a joyful disposition and he meets many people freely. After that meeting, he goes to the temple outside the gates of the palace.

The prince planned to take the king as prisoner and force him to declare the former as the king.

But one of the close associates of the prince was bribed by the minister of the kingdom to the west of the kingdom of Yasasakta. Through that man the information about the plan of kidnapping the king Yasasakta was leaked to the enemy king.

They waited for the opportunity in the neighborhood.

When the prince Yasassikhara took his father as prisoner and was trying to transfer him to his selected place, men of the enemy king overpowered them. A battle ensued between them.

Finally, the well prepared enemy men outsmarted the prince's men by the advantage of surprise element. They took both the king and prince as prisoners in one stroke. The arrogant royalty gave away their kingdom to their neighboring king on a platter."

Charudas stopped his narration for taking a glass of water.

The audience was spellbound with the twists and turns of the story.

They asked the story teller for one more. Those who were not interested too needed a lullaby to get sleep, so they also joined others in forcing Charudas to exert further.

So, not so reluctant Charudas began again.

"In the village of Seethasamudra, two householders Suravarma and Athisuravarma lived one beside the other. They were in the habit of quarrelling with each other for every big and small issue.

They were envious of each other.

Suravarma had a mango tree in his house. It was on the border between the two houses. As if by design, big branches of that tree bent towards the other's house. That year, it started bearing fruits and most of the fruits were on the other side of the border wall. Without any action on his part most of the fruits fell on the side of Athisuravarma. In the beginning, his wife returned the fruits back to Suravarma. Yet he was not satisfied with the count of fruits given back to him. He told neighbors that Athisuravarma had kept many of his fruits and that he gave only a small part back to him. The latter since then did not return the fruits that fell in his yard. There were allegations and counter allegations against each other.

Then one day, Suravarma called a laborer and engaged him to cut away the branches of the mango tree which were bent towards his neighbor's house. As most of the big branches were on the other side, after some days the tree withered and was dead ultimately.

Suravarma was envious of the riches of his neighbor. His neighbor became rich as his wife got share of properties from her father, as the only daughter of him, after his sudden death, a few days before.

Suravarma consulted many of his friends to become rich by some easy means. One of his friends suggested gambling as an easy way to get rich. He went to a gambling house and was cheated of his money. His wife scolded him and he vowed never to enter a gambling house again.

One day his brother in law came from the village to his house, with fruits and vegetables grown in his farm. He heard about the nagging worry of his brother in law, from his sister. He thought over the matter for some time. After lunch and rest he was prepared to go back to his village.

At that time his sister asked him whether he could think of some solution to her husband's worry.

Her brother told her he could do some business of his liking and if he were lucky he could become a richer man than his neighbor. But his brother in law did not favor that, as it would take many years before one could become a successful businessman. There would be competition from the peers in the line. He had to overcome that. So, there was no certainty of that.

His brother in law then suggested that for his problem the only solution could be to seek the help of some proved god-man.

Suravarma then asked his brother in law if he knew any such person.

His brother in law thought over and advised him to go to the temple on the hillock beside his village and meet the priest, who meditates there. He looked at his sister and smiled. She knew that her brother did not believe in such affairs. However to keep his brother-in-law happy, he told that easy method to him. He thought if his brother in law was lucky the priest would give him some suitable advice.

Next day, early in the morning Suravarma started towards the temple on the hillock alone.

When he reached the temple, the priest was in prayer. Suravarma waited till he finished his prayer and then prostrated before him.

The priest blessed and asked him the reason for his sudden arrival there.

Suravarma explained his necessity for riches. The priest smiled and then asked if he could meditate for a number of days till his desire was fulfilled.

Suravarma was now determined. He knew that there was a way out for his problem. So however hard the solution was, he was prepared to pursue that path. He told the same to the priest.

He sent word to his wife through a cowherd boy about his going into meditation till his desire was fulfilled. He then went into the forest far above on that hillock and began meditation as directed by the priest.

But the information about the meditation of Suravarma reached Athisuravarma through the cowherd boy, whom he forced to reveal the message.

So Athisuravarma too met the priest and went to the same forest and began severe penance as advised by him.

Number of days passed and the families of the competitor-aspirants were worried about them.

But the Suravarma and Athisuravarma continued without break and doubt about the result of their meditation.

One day at last the Lord appeared before Suravarma and asked him about his requirement.

He replied, "My Lord, I request whatever my neighbor wants, please grant me double that?"

The Lord then appeared before Athisuravarma and asked him as to what he wanted from Him.

Athisuravarma then with a smile asked the Lord, "My Lord, please tell me what my neighbor there asked of you?"

The Lord gave the information he wanted.

Then Athisuravarma thought over for a few moments.

He asked the Lord with a wicked smile, "My Lord then, you kindly take away half of my wealth. That is my humble desire."

The Lord then made their desires fulfilled. So Athisuravarma got his riches reduced to half and for all his troubles. Suravarma became poor, losing all he had.

"The envy filled neighbors thus got the well-deserved judgment by the Lord."

Charudas stopped his narration.

The group of visitors then had a nice siesta.

When they were ready to leave that place, a swami with his disciples came there. The visitors were surprised to see an ascetic at that place, where as they know only persons with mundane desires, that is those who were in search of treasures, were seen.

After the first reaction, some of them prostrated at the feet of the swami. The swami was none other than swami Anandagiri of Brindavan.

Those who did not take cognizance of the swami were Vacra on the one extreme and Charudas on the other. Vacra professionally could not yield to such soft attitudes.

Charudas on the other hand came a long way from such 'irrational' ways.

The ascetic and his disciples then occupied the stone-seats for meditation. The other group left that place into the ashram.

* * *

The ashram wore a festive look, with so many aspirants roaming around with purposeful and sincere outlook.

The evening gave a new dimension with beautifully lit lights all around the ashram. They lit wicks of cotton wool kept in earthen cups filled with vegetable oil. The disciples of the swami took special care to light the small temple like erection they made for the auspicious occasion of one of the important days of the month.

There was bhajan and prayer by those who were interested in the occasion. The disciples of the swami took part in cooking and serving the night meal.

The full moon gave special elegance to the ambience.

The disciples sat in a semicircle around the swami outside the ashram. As was the practice, the swami began a story from a religious book or some incident of moral principle for the guidance of the disciples.

"Once it happened that the celestial singer Narada went to Dwaraka where Lord Krishna resided. He asked the Lord if there was any merit in visiting great saints."

The other aspirants who heard the beginning of the story too wanted to know the answer to that question of Narada. So they began collecting around the disciples as a second circle.

The swami continued, "Lord Krishna did not answer him. He asked the divine singer to go to Nasik town and repeat the query to a beetle living in a particular place full of cow dung. Narada went there and could easily locate the beetle, happily moving around in the cow dung.

He asked the beetle, "Is there any benefit in visiting great saints?"

At once the beetle fell motionless and died.

Narada felt sad and returned to Lord Krishna in disappointment.

The Lord asked him, "Why Narada, what made you so sad and disappointed?"

Narada replied, "My Lord, as directed by you I went to the beetle in Nasik. But the moment I asked it about benefits of visiting great saints, it fell dead. I am very sorry to have become the cause of its death."

Lord Krishna smiled and said, "Narada, don't you worry about that. You please go to Hastinapura and meet a sparrow in the temple there. Please repeat the question to it."

It took a few days before he reached Hastinapura. He could easily locate the sparrow in the temple, as it came forward the moment it saw the saint.

The divine singer repeated his question to it.

Again the same thing happened. The sparrow died at once without a cause, as if the words had potency to kill.

Narada returned to the Lord with heavy heart.

He then told him, "My Lord, enough of this killing spree. Kindly you yourself give the answer to my question."

But the Lord told him, "My dear Narada, its nothing. You are not responsible for their death. Now for this last time, you do as I say. You please go eastward to Varanasi, and meet the new born prince and ask him this question."

Narada said, "My Lord, this time it's certain I will be taken to task for killing the prince."

Lord Krishna said, "This time he would not die. Please go as I said."

Narada went to Varanasi leisurely. He was not in a hurry this time. He prayed in the temple of Lord Viswanath. Later he went to the king and told him that he wanted to see the prince. He told those words hesitantly.

The king was happy to receive the divine singer in his palace. He honored the saint in all prescribed ways and finally took him to the place where the newborn prince was.

The infant prince smiled at seeing the saint.

Narada fondled the boy for some time to procrastinate the tragedy.

At last he asked the prince why it was beneficial to see a great saint.

The price at once became a divine person in a luminous body.

He replied, "Holy saint, I am the sparrow which died after your visit to the temple. I am the beetle which died in similar circumstances. After seeing you I had the fortune of taking birth as a sparrow, after dying as a beetle. Again I died as a sparrow to take the higher birth of a prince. Now I had the fortune of becoming a divine person from the state of a prince. This all happened as I was lucky to see you, a great saint, in my previous lives and now.

The prince turned divine person, prostrated before the divine singer and then left for heavenly abode.

Narada now satisfied with the answer provided by the series of incidents, returned to Lord Krishna. He thanked him for the ingenious way the Lord answered his query."

The swami began his prayer, indicating the closer of the session.

The swami and his disciples went into the interiors of the ashram, where they were provided a separate accommodation. All others went to the places provided for them.

Ramsaran went out of the ashram to ease. He reached a place away from the habitation and close to the edge of hill. Beyond that it was a valley, but a barricade was there for safety. When he was busy with that, he heard revolver shots close to him. He saw Vacra at a distance, with revolver in his hand and a wicked smile on his face. Ramsaran thought over quickly. He did not know why Vacra had animosity against him. To save himself Ramsaran picked a big stone lying there and threw it at Vacra. The latter got hit on the left leg.

He then advanced forward with anger and tried to push Ramsaran over the barricade. With sudden impact, he fell over the barrier and saved himself by clutching the barricade rafter from falling down into the abyss.

Vacra though limping tried to undo the grip of Ramsaran from the support. As he came close to him, Ramsaran in a sudden move snatched away the revolver from the other and fired a blind shot. The bullet had hit Vacra on the right hand and he fell down at once. While falling down he caught hold of the leg of Ramsaran and thus took him down with him into the depths of no return.

XVI

The swami and his disciples, Charudas and others and Saral and his colleagues started on their further trek.

Veera and Nishit wanted to stay back at the ashram for rest and preparation.

The surroundings had become pleasant. All the plants around the footpath were in full bloom. A number of trees had their branches full of varied fruits which the visitors had never seen before.

The aspirants felt they were in a different world, a better world or was it heaven, they thought.

Many of the vacant places on the way on either side of the pathway were lined up with flat stones good for sitting. At some places holy men sat on those stones and were praying.

The swami said that sun was seen there only in the early morning. Holy men pray to the Sun God then. Later on the sun was not seen, but only the light indicates that it was day.

At midday the swami asked his disciples to halt at a broad clean place to eat whatever was available. He asked them to bring fruits and flowers of the trees.

They ate the fruits and drank the nectar like honey from the flowers. Other visitors followed suit.

They were refreshed more than when they ate usual mid-day meals.

They were on the path for higher regions again.

As the atmosphere was so pleasant, they did not feel like taking rest then.

The entire group of a score of aspirants continued on their path with various thoughts passing through their minds. Some discussed them amongst them and some others kept to themselves.

Charudas was pondering over the words of the person who belonged to the ashram about the quality of worthiness to reach higher regions of the mountain.

The swami looked at him with a smile.

He said, "My dear friend, I know you are anxious to know about the deservedness of a person to reach higher regions of this mountain."

Charudas was flabbergasted.

He looked around to share his surprise with others and uttered in amazement, "Revered swami, that is exactly what is nagging me right now. Without knowing about that what purpose does it serve to go further on trek? Kindly let us know about that."

The swami began, "I would narrate a story to make that clear. A few centuries back, those were the days when more good people were seen than bad ones, in a city there lived a dancer-girl of repute. She was visited by many rich men and courtiers of the royal court. She became very rich in a short time and even at a very young age. She was charming and good in her trade and intelligent too. She lived in a large bungalow away from the humdrum of the city.

Not far from that bungalow, a holy-man had an ashram and he lived there with his small band of disciples. The holy-man and his followers used to pass in front of the bungalow of the dancer-girl to reach the houses in the city for begging for food. As they were mendicants they would not keep money or cook foods for themselves, like householders. They used to wear orange robes as ordained for such persons.

The dancer-girl used to see them, passing in front of her palace every day. Either the holy-man or his disciples used to go for begging food in the households. She used to compare her life with those holy persons. She knew she would not deserve good after-world position, as her profession was to please each and every visitor to her palace with dance and entertainment. She was a lowly person looked down in the society, though rich. She might not go to heaven like those holy-men who pass by her palace every day. Her mind always used to think about those holy-men and heaven only. She aspired to get a similar opportunity either in this birth or if not possible at least in the next one.

Now the holy-man, that guru, while passing in front of the palace of the dancer-girl used to think about her and her bad ways. He used to pity her for her immoral deeds. He was sure that she would not deserve heaven after her death. The holy man day after day used to remember her and her immorality. He even used to pray for her.

After many years the holy-man died. Then an unexpected thing, unexpected by the holy-man, happened. To receive his astral body, servants of hell arrived.

Same day the woman of bad morals, the dancer-girl too died. And for receiving her heavenly people came.

The holy-man was surprised and accosted the men from hell and asked, "How is that you are taking me to hell? I am a holy man and during my entire life I was practicing spiritual ways and was God minded. Not only that, those heavenly people are taking that woman of bad morals to heaven. There must be some mistake in this. The action was reversed by mistake, I think."

One of the men from hell laughed and replied, "There was no mistake at all. Though you were a holy-man, as you lived near the palace of that woman, your mind was engrossed with her immoral life. You were thinking of her only. But that woman though pursuing a bad way of life as a profession, she was thinking of you people and your holy ways of living. Her mind was always after that kind of life and engrossed in good thoughts. So she deserved heaven. It is not the way you live, but it is the attitude and mental preoccupation that counts. One's heart must be pure to deserve better life after death."

The swami now asked the listeners if they appreciated what was told by the person of the ashram, which they left a few hours before. As told by him it was the well-deserved that were destined for greater benefits, be it mundane or other worldly.

The aspirants agreed to the logic of the moral story. Each one of them began assessing his level of attainment in that quality. But it appeared for everybody that he had all the required qualities for higher attainment.

The swami with a broad smile said to the aspirants, "What I told now is about the after-world benefits, befitting such a person who had achieved required stature. Don't you want to know about the benefits derived in the present world for the selfless work of such persons?"

They all wanted to know and expressed so in one voice.

The holy-man began, "In the days of guru-prophet Adishankara, there lived an old widow who was very poor. As all her people abandoned her, she lived alone begging for food in the village where she had been brought up, married and widowed later.

As long as she was energetic enough she used to work and earn money for her maintenance. When she could not work anymore she began begging. But after some days, even that she was not able to do. She remained at home and if anybody was kind enough to give, she would eat.

On one morning, Adishankara, who was a boy but an ascetic, went around the village for begging food. The ascetics would not remain in one place for long. They go away to another place before they get attached to anything or anybody at that place. A mendicant fixes certain number of households to beg. If he gets food in those households he eats otherwise he forgoes food on that day.

On that day, during the course of visiting the households Adishankara went to the house of that old widow. He asked for food, standing in front of the house. Nobody replied. He again made his voice heard. But the old woman could not come out as she was not clad properly due to lack of a sari. She wore a torn sari and was not in a position to come out. She did not have anything to give to the mendicant, except dried amala, a kind of fruit. On repeated requests by the mendicant, she came out and gave that dried fruit to him, while feeling very much embarrassed. Adishankara took and bit that fruit. He blessed her though she did not ask for anything.

Then a miracle happened. Her entire house was filled with golden amalas.

She was blessed for the fulfillment of her earthly desires, as she deserved that."

Some of the visitors had a doubt—was it possible though they were deserved they might not be blessed yet? Otherwise how was that possible for them not to experience any indications though they were deserved? They knew that they were deserved otherwise they would not have come that far.

So, one of them asked the swami "Holy sir, is it possible for somebody though he was deserved, no external indication might be forthcoming, but could be assessed by others as deserved for fulfillment?"

The swami answered "Yes, there are cases where others identified the greatness of such persons, though they might not be aware of their greatness."

"Sir, kindly narrate that incident to us."

"That was during the times of Mahabharat. The royal family of Pandavas headed by Dharmaraja, performed a great ritual. After successful completion of that ritual, they fed many people for days together. Many wise persons and saints blessed them for their charities.

One of those days, it happened that Dharmaraja while supervising the feeding of Brahmins, observed a squirrel rolling on the slushy ground where the visitors washed their hands after taking food. He saw that one side of its body was of golden hue. The king could not contain his surprise at the peculiar act of the squirrel and also the color of its body. And he asked the squirrel for the reason of it. He was prepared to feed that squirrel with the best condiments of the royal kitchen, if it wanted to partake. It was not necessary for it to roam around on those slushy grounds full of leftover food.

But the squirrel replied, "Great king, I had not come for taking part in the feast given here. You might have observed my body half of which is of golden hue."

"Yes, I saw that. What is the reason for this peculiar phenomenon?"

"Oh king, when I came to know that you are performing this great ritual and feeding so many people, I thought of making rest of my body of golden hue."

"But how? What is the relationship between the feast and making your body golden?"

"I am sorry to say My King, I am disappointed. I could not fulfill my desire. When the poor Brahmin of that town in the east, performed his small ritual and fed people to the extent he could afford, I rubbed my body with the mud of those who ate and washed there, and my body turned gold. But it was only half work done, as the slush was not sufficient as the men fed were small in number. I wanted to repeat the same here to render my body golden in full. But I could not. You know the reason, My King. The action and merit go hand in hand in deserved proportion."

The squirrel left the King who bent his head in shame, his pride of giving charities shattered to pieces.

Thus the merits of one's actions would not depend on the magnitude and could not be judged by him. The resultant indications are elsewhere."

The swami concluded and they continued their journey.

After a few hours, the swami and disciples stopped at a place where some people were in meditation. They all appeared like saints with long beards and closed eyes, without any apparent motion of the body.

The swami and disciples joined them. Charudas and Sudhama too stayed with them.

* * *

All others of the group proceeded further. They tried sitting to meditate on earlier occasions but failed. They thought it was not an exercise for people like them. So they kept going, not stopping for the group of the swami.

It was getting dark but soon there was light. The light emanated from the stones lying on either side of the pathway and also flowers of some trees. They had no difficulty in walking.

They walked and walked, but could not reach any village on the way. However there was no difficulty for food and shelter. The fruits and flowers were available throughout. As the atmosphere was pleasant there was no necessity for any shelter. There were no wild animals to be afraid of either.

They walked for many hours, but it appeared there was no progress.

They discussed and finally came to the conclusion that they might have missed the correct path. They must be going around the same path repeatedly as they found similar land marks on their way again and again.

Next morning, they started again after a night's rest.

After passing some distance they heard some voices at a distance. Presently they saw a few visitors whom they had not met before. They belonged to another group.

They appeared disappointed and were not enthusiastic of the trek any more.

Saral asked one of them, "Friends, where from you, people are coming?"

"We are coming from different places. But now we don't know where we are going. We have been going around the place, but there was no progress. Many times we reached the same place."

"You too think that you missed the path?"

"Are you too in the same predicament?"

"Yes, we were in fact a bigger group. There was a swami and his disciples in the group. But we left them behind, to reach the destination fast. And now we are lost. Had we continued with the swami, we would not have faced this situation."

Then one amongst them suggested, "We may meet some such holy person on our path. So it is better we continue our trek."

Others agreed and they all again started with renewed spirit.

After going for some distance, they saw some saintly men meditating on elevated flat stones.

One of the new visitors rushed towards the nearest saint. He asked him about the route to reach the higher regions of the mountain.

The sage did not reply. Even though he repeated the query there was no reply.

Saral asked him not to venture any more attempts. The saint might not like it. Instead of a reply he might get a curse, if he was incensed for the disturbance.

Ultimately, they decided that they would enquire any saintly person, who was not in meditation.

So they abandoned the idea of asking those saints and proceeded further.

At around midday, they saw a saintly man picking fruits and flowers from the trees.

Saral asked him after greeting with reverence, "Holy sir, we have been going around this place since a few days. We missed the correct route, I suppose. Will you kindly help us?"

The holy man smiled benevolently and said, "My dear friend, it happens so. Up to this place you could all come because of your good fate. Now unless you make yourself fit you cannot go further."

"But sir, how would we become fit for further progress?"

"For that you seek the help of God sincerely. When you are fit you would go further."

With those words the saint walked away hastily.

Saral said to his colleagues, "Now we have to follow the words of the saint."

"It appears there is no other way, as we cannot even go back. It is equally difficult." The other man said.

They all settled on the ground, well carpeted with the green grass.

XVII

Swami and disciples with Charudas and Sudhama following them proceeded through the garden-like terrain once more.

They invariably halted morning, midday and evening at the places of meditation. Charudas improved his ability in meditation with the help of Sudhama. Sudhama was almost an adept in that.

The nights were not dark as there was sufficient light emitted by the stones and flowers on the way.

Charudas imagined that he saw tigers coming close to him and Sudhama. Sometimes ghosts appeared in front of them. It happened many times thus. They were taken aback.

Charudas was terrified in the beginning.

But they observed that swami or his disciples were not affected.

The swami clarified them that what they saw were all illusions to divert less resolute persons.

After going further, they observed at a distance some other groups of people too trekking up on other routes.

Now they could discern the shape of the mountain, as the contours of the mountain could be made out at the higher altitude.

Further the different routes appeared to be coming closer, as they could see at a distance many other visitors on their way. Still the persons belonging to each group stayed together though they moved forward in the same direction and with the same purpose. They developed affinity amongst themselves. They did not venture to keep faith in strangers after so many days of travel. They experienced harsh realities on their way.

Later when it was getting dark and the dim light illumined the surroundings, they reached a level ground which appeared as if it was there for those visitors for night's rest.

The cool breeze had taken away all the vestiges of tiredness from their bodies. They became refreshed. The fruits and flowers helped to quench their hunger and thirst.

They slipped into deep slumber on that plain ground carpeted by smooth green grass, without any disturbance or danger.

When they woke up early dawn next day, they saw a great glow on top of the mountain, which was not far away. The glow was like sun. Some thought they were close to the sun. But the glow was not hot like the rays of sun. It was cool and pleasing. It was not moon either. The glow was not far away in the sky like the sun or moon. It appeared approachable.

The visitors were jerked into action. They finished morning ablutions fast. The journey was resumed now with renewed enthusiasm.

The glow was inviting. It beckoned them to it. They even forgot to eat and proceeded without any other thought. It continued thus for some hours. Then, the glow disappeared as suddenly as it appeared to them.

Having seen and concentrated on the glow for a few hours, when it disappeared, they felt as if they were left in darkness. It was fathomless darkness.

After some time they felt the pangs of hunger and remembered the fruits on the trees around. They plucked some and ate. They drank the flower-nectar.

Some of the visitors as well as the disciples of the swami tried to ask him about the phenomena. But he was tight lipped and appeared to be in a trance like condition.

They saw ahead of them some others still going as if in a trance with gaze fixed on something not far away from them. They might be seeing the glow.

Even some in the group of swami, saw the glow again after many hours and pushed forward on the way once more. Swami was in trance and sat cross legged on the mat like grass.

This hide and seek went on for a number of times. Various groups of visitors some before and some others behind the group of swami, went on thus for hours together.

Now it was certain that some great power was beckoning them to it. They did not know what that was and how it was going to be useful, but its attraction was such that they were not able to resist the temptation to proceed towards that power.

The people in pursuit of the glow were of various descriptions, some were like saints and some others looked ordinary, without any outward indications of distinction.

It appeared to be a one way trek as nobody was seen returning from the top of the mountain with fulfillment of desire or without.

With the kind of experiences they had and the nights merged into day by the presence of light always, they lost discrimination of day and night in that glorious land.

*   *   *

With the appearance of glow of light selectively to one here and another there, groups had split away into individual seekers each being unaware of others experience of this phenomenon.

The individual aspirants moved ahead guided by the glow upward, towards the top of the mountain.

Those who were on the path in advance, sometimes found themselves lagging behind due to the lack of guidance and vice versa. So now it had become an individual effort and a different experience from person to person.

They reached the top of the mountain, which was called in common parlance 'sixth camp', one by one.

* * *

In a state of high consciousness each reached the pinnacle of the mountain, which was a level ground covered with emerald like green grass. Now, no one was conscious of the presence of others.

After going further, each saw the glow manifesting into a human form. They could see it as an outline of human form filled with the light and seated on a high pedestal.

Wherever he saw the form, each aspirant stood stuck to the ground there and paid obeisance to him.

* * *

Swami saw the form beckoning him, the glow filled outline of human form.

The celestial being asked the swami in thunder like resonating voice "My dear one, what do you desire?"

Swami found himself out of that trance which engulfed him till then.

He replied. He desired something unconnected to the mundane affairs.

The formless form raised his hand and swami heard an approving smile and then "Thadastu"

The index finger of the extended hand pointed down towards the ground.

The form with glow disappeared for him and swami found the entire surroundings changed in a moment. He was no more on the Green Mountain. He found himself in his ashram of Brindavan to his amazement.

*   *   *

Each of the disciples of the swami had got his desire, hidden deep in mind, granted and then transported away to the place suited for materialization of the desire.

*   *   *

Charudas and Sudhama got blessings for their desires and so is the case with many of others group, however one not knowing about the other.

The endless affair of blessings for the deserved pilgrims went on and on. It has become a perennial phenomenon.

Part-II

I

The fall was quick. Vacra plunged fast to a few lengths, but was saved because of foliage. The trees there had more foliage and creepers due to the conditions prevailing at those altitudes of the mountain. He was stopped from falling down further because of a large branch, on which he was saddled safely. Vacra was dazed and steadied himself by catching an upward grown branch. He felt a sudden pain in the arm. A few moments before he was shot by Ramsaran and luckily for him the bullet had not gone deep in but he was bleeding. Ramsaran was not seen anywhere nearby. He might have fallen down further to his death. He tore off a piece of cloth from his shirt and tried to use it as a bandage for his wound. He could not tie the ends with one hand, however much he tried. He could ultimately press the cloth piece against the wound to stop bleeding. In his anxiety, he plucked a few leaves he saw around him, some from the creepers and some others from the tree on branches of which he rested now. He squeezed them and used that juice to apply on the wound.

Vacra closed his eyes for a few moments.

He heard sound of leaves disturbed at a distance. He was in the midst of foliage of trees and creepers. When he half opened his eyes, he saw a python advancing towards him. The python was double his size in length, but not stout enough to gulp him through its mouth, Vacra thought. But he remembered that python could also grab and crush the victim by encircling him and eat slowly. It halted at the minute sound made by him while adjusting himself.

After a while the python began moving towards him again. He could see its glassy eyes and grey and light brown scales on its body. He felt for the knife in the scabbard at his back.

Vacra was not a person of timid nature, but he knew when to face enemy squarely and when to leave him alone. Now, he was to leave that place any how to go home. So there was no point in attacking python to save himself. He could as well escape by moving away from that jungle creature.

Vacra without wasting time further caught hold of a thick creeper with his other hand that not wounded and began sliding down.

He made a good distance from his enemy and looked down to find level ground full of grass covering it. He slid to the ground.

He felt hungry. He did not eat since the last meal at the ashram, the previous night. He made effort to get up while looking around for any fruit bearing trees. He saw some fruits on a tree at a distance and dragged on towards that. Nevertheless he was not sure of their edibility. When he was in two minds to eat or not he saw a monkey eating a fruit on a branch on the other side of the tree.

Vacra picked up a dry branch of a tree lying nearby and dislodged a few fruits by hitting the tree branches. The fruits were tasty and looked like mangoes but not sweet enough like a mango fruit. While picking the fruits on the ground, Vacra to his great joy and surprise found his revolver lying by a large stone on one side of the pathway. He rushed to it and grabbed it in his hands. He kissed it as if it were a pet. That was a second time he lost his weapon and recovered again.

After finishing the fruits, he took a gulp of water from the clear stream of water running down the rocks close by.

Now he began trekking down again, choosing a path like clear place. There was no sign of existing pathways like elsewhere, as nobody ever came that way. He was not sure whether the path leads to the ground below. He could not find any habitation or people below, because of the thick grown vegetation and trees, impeding visibility from that height.

After trekking down for a few hours, though not with certain hope, he stopped to rest under a tree. It was a clear place. He picked a flat stone lying close by and used it as a pillow. He lied down while his tired knee joints made adjusting sounds.

He closed his eyes while cool breeze comforted his limbs. The sun was going down the western arc and it was well past midday.

He slept for long with the body in shambles, after the hectic downward journey.

With the noise of birds reaching home for the evening, he opened eyes and had to close them at once due to the dazzling light that targeted his face.

He moved aside and looked at the source of the light.

He was flabbergasted to see rays of colored light emanating from the small stones on the upright surface of the mountain, facing the west. The sun rays fell on the pebbles embedded on the exterior of the mountain, opposite him and gave out piercing rays of colored light.

It did not take much time for him to infer that they were some kind of precious stones. Nobody must have passed that way till then or noticed them. Otherwise he would not have the exclusive chance of seeing them and owning them in a short while. In other words by then nothing would have remained there, had some people passed that way. Alternatively, he thought the precious stones must have surfaced by rains lashing on the mountain, which was not unusual. The earth covered surface must have opened up after many such seasons.

He looked around to make sure he was alone for the loot and moved closer to the stones.

He surmised he could not see them before because the stones would not shine unless light rays fell on them.

Vacra picked up a sharp stone lying there and began extracting the colored stones which would become gems after cutting. He concentrated on bigger ones which he knew fetch higher value as they were of higher rating of carats.

He made enough collection of those gemstones that he could carry with him. He must also make them concealed so that nobody by any chance sees them, when he changes clothes or un-robes himself for washing.

He already made up his mind to reach home at the earliest. He made a mental picture of the place and wanted to remember the route to that place after reaching the ground. He might make another trip for replenishment of gemstones later.

Vacra felt assured of the safety of the valuables, as he had a revolver with him luckily for him. He thought God only was guiding him now. This trip to the mountain was like a pilgrimage. Before this adventure, God was only an idea to him; an idea to bargain with for something—'*Quid Pro Co.*'

Now he was sure that God only showed him the gems. He only returned to him the revolver he lost, during the tussle with Ramsaran. He thanked God for all that.

While thinking and planning, he came down the mountain terrain a few miles, without feeling the strain. His mind was engrossed in the joyful thoughts of the life he was going to lead later. That worked like a tonic for him; like an effective drink. An effective drink, ahha!. He remembered his favorite drink. But how he would get it now? He had plenty of resources with him now. He looked around to find hopefully even a toddy drink. But there were no traces of toddy trees in that terrain. He quenched his thirst by drinking water available there.

Suddenly he heard some voices. In no time, he saw some cowherd boys enjoying playing with each other.

They were surprised to see him, who was dressed so differently and looked outlandish.

He asked one of them from which village they came there. That boy replied they were from 'Ramgarh' village.

He knew umpteen villages with that name. That thought brought a smile on his face. The village of his childhood times which also goes by that name 'Ramgarh' came to his mind.

He was seven years old at that time. He lost his father. He died of some disease, pain in the back. The pain was incessant. He remembered the scene of his father crying, while he shaved himself. He, his mother and brother were watching, not knowing what to do. It was unusual for elderly people to cry, that too for a male member of the family.

When his father died, the body was kept on an old string cot. Out of curiosity he went near the body. His mother sat at a distance from the body and was crying loudly. Some others and his uncles were busy talking with each other. His father was lying there without motion. Then he saw some ants on his left foot. They must be biting him. But he was not moving his leg. At that time, one of his uncles catching hold of his arm pulled him away. He felt it odd to note that nobody cared for his father. When asked about the ants, his uncle replied that his father was no more. That brought tears to him.

His mother was crying for days together. He and his brother were taken care of by their aunts, father's sisters.

One day his aunt bathed them near the well, located in the backyard. She poured cold water drawn from the well on their young bodies. They were not habituated to cold water bath, that too open in the air. They shivered. But aunt was busy with other thoughts and did not notice or cared like their mother. After that they suffered severe cold for a few days. They could not speak, as the voice was choked due to the cold.

That was about 'Ramgarh.'

The cowherd boys looked at him in surprise as he looked absented minded and laughed in himself. He was weather beaten and looked like a mad man. They laughed amongst themselves looking at the odd person.

Vacra gained momentum, now that he knew he was close to some village. From there he could reach his place without much delay. He was rich now and could afford to spend money for his needs well.

He would become someone noticed by everybody, might be in his village or elsewhere. He touched the bundle containing the gemstones with his hand lightly. They were there to reassure him.

He would buy a bungalow and live happily with wife and children. But as he remembered there was no big bungalow in his village, not big enough for him now. Moreover those villagers might not like his new life style. So doubly it was necessary for him to shift to a better place. But small places always have people with prying eyes and he does not want to be noticed for the wrong reason. He must avoid known people, known him before. It boils down to big places or say cities. Anyway he must know how much he was worth now. He would have to go to a jeweler for checking the gemstones for their value. Of course he would have to double check with another, as you cannot keep faith in only one in such matters. He knew his cousin Badri was good in gems selection. But he would not believe him any more after he tried to cheat him on one earlier occasion.

He himself was not a gem of a man either. But he was a changed man, after the trip to the Green Mountain. His confidence doubled after he was bestowed with gifts of precious stones by God. He saw people of various kinds of nature on the way. They were after the treasures. What kind of treasures they got, he did not know. He could not reach the top, however. He had no regrets now on that score. In a way Ramsaran, poor boy was instrumental for his riches. He might have tried to kill him. But the urge on the way to mountain top was combative and competitive. He knew many politicians got killed before they reached successful careers, by rivals. They were very ambitious and cruel too. He was in no way worse than those.

Vacra reached the village Ramgarh. He felt it strange to move alone without his aids. Except at his home town, he was always attended by a few of his professional buddies.

He went to a barber shop situated on the main road. He checked himself in the mirror. He could not recognize his own face. He got shaved and groomed with a haircut. He had to pay to the barber. He searched in the shoulder bag. He could find a few coins. He placed those into the out stretched hand of the barber, who returned them at once with a sneer. Vacra's eyes flashed in anger and he lifted up his garment to uncover the revolver. The barber trembled in fear and crouched back behind the last chair in that corner of the shop.

Vacra slowly scanned the entrance and the road beyond. There were no visitors and road too was not crowded yet. He looked towards the barber who continued to be in stupor for the sudden happening.

He moved over to the road and once on the road walked away briskly to avoid any repercussions. It was past eight o'clock and the street lights were on. He reached the bus stand. No buses were plying then. He found a small tea-shop close to the bus stand. After eating rotis and dal, he managed to get a place to sleep for the night.

Vacra woke up early in the morning and finished ablutions. He had tea in the shop. He walked over to the bus stand.

A bus was already there and passengers were getting into it feverishly. Vacra too vigorously joined the crowd and got in. He pushed aside a few men and occupied a seat.

By midday the bus halted at a place called 'Chota Bareile.'

Vacra got down and began walking on the main road looking for a jeweler shop. He did not have money even to eat a sumptuous meal. After a while he saw board of a jeweler shop. Vacra picked out one small diamond from the bag and kept it in his front pocket.

He looked inside the shop and found the shopkeeper alone who was smiling as he entered.

Vacra sat on the stool in front of the wooden counter. The shopkeeper raised his eye brows for a moment as a question mark. Vacra slowly pulled out the diamond and opened his fist with the glittering gem in it. The shopkeeper stretched out his hand and Vacra dropped it into his hand.

He asked, "How much do you offer?"

The shopkeeper concentrated his looks on the gem for a moment and rubbed it with a cloth lightly.

Without answering him, the latter opened the drawers of the cupboard, pulled out a small bundle of currency notes and kept them on the counter.

Vacra after seeing the money, revised his opinion of selling the gem, bending forward he grabbed the gemstone back from the shopkeeper and in a flash took the money too.

He got up and before the shopkeeper opened his mouth, pulled out the revolver from the undergarment and pointed out at him. The shopkeeper stunned into silence, crouched under the counter looking at Vacra with eyes wide open in fear.

Vacra looked out of the door on to the road. The way was clear. He then kept the firearm back inside and walked out with a warning look for the shopkeeper. Once on the road Vacra with a beaming face, walked briskly away from that place.

After walking some distance he saw a bus just started to move. People were hanging at the door to enter the over crowded bus. Vacra ran after the bus pushed others away and entered the bus. He then made place for himself by pushing the passengers aside as his wont.

At the next stop, he alighted. The place was good enough for his purpose. He was hungry. But before that he wanted to change into a better dress, for a respectable treatment.

He selected two pairs of pants and shirts to suit his purpose and put on one of the dresses he chose now. He paid the cloth shop fellow as he could afford now.

Vacra then chose an eatery, to assuage his hunger. He ate to his heart's content.

Now a happy and satisfied Vacra, walked towards the bus stand. He got into the bus which was bound to his place.

* * *

He reached home. His wife and son were happy to receive him. It was two months back he left home. She began asking many questions. He told her how he fought with enemies in adverse situations and won treasures after many days. He used all his talents in story telling to convince her. He was an adept in such a craft, in dealing with the questioning by police people.

After washing and refreshing, he went into the bedroom. The bag containing the gemstones was to be kept in a safe place. He had a place where he usually puts his earnings, after every exploit. That was behind the mirror, where he had a secret cupboard. He placed the valuables in that safe and locked it.

He woke up by the time it was evening. He went to shop for his next day's trip to Mumbai.

He planned to set himself in a suitable way in the future life. He must have money for that. The gemstones were to be exchanged for cash. He must become legally rich.

He knew that the gemstones were to be declared to the authorities legally. He might get a small portion of their value officially. So he had to avoid that route. He planned to go to Mumbai, sell them batch by batch and then establish himself as a businessman there. Thus he could make the money 'white' in business parlance.

He of course felt the absence of his assistants. The show would have been more real and easy to play. Unfortunately they were left behind on the mountain. How they would fare with the situations prevailing there, he could not imagine. It was really a tough life out there.

The gemstones were of different sizes and types. The values would be different. He wanted to find their value at good markets of Mumbai and Surat. He had to carefully deal with this affair. He did not have much knowledge in that field, particularly in the case of uncut diamonds. He could not rely on some unknown person for that. The weights of cut ones that emerge from mined gems might be difficult assess. He might be deceived in that.

So he must offer to sell each uncut piece one by one to different shops or a small number at a time, depending on the sizes. It was alright even if he got lesser dough for the uncut pieces. He must also avoid the evil eyes of police and criminals.

Next day, he loaded the suit case with his clothes for a two weeks trip. He took out the bag containing gemstones from the secret place and concealed it in a secret pouch in the lower portion of the suit case. Over that all his clothes were packed well. He then locked the suitcase. He also carried a chain and padlock to fix the suitcase under the seat after boarding the train.

By evening, he was at the railway station with his suitcase of high value. It took much time to leave his wife and son again after so many days of separation. He told her that he was on his business trip and after his return from Mumbai he would take them to that great city for good.

He reached Delhi and from there entrained for Mumbai.

At Mumbai, he stayed in a hotel near V.T. The hotel was reasonably comfortable and reputed. He made enquiries before checking in. He must take care not to attract the attention of wrong people.

He went round the city to check the correct place for selling the gemstones.

At last he chose a jewelers shop near Bandra. He entered the shop hesitantly. He did not know how to start the dialogue. He was shown a seat by a smiling young man sitting at the counter.

Vacra pulled out the purse containing the gemstones from vest pocket.

"I want to sell this."

He said in a casual way, while picking out one gemstone from the purse.

The shop fellow called someone, who was one of the other two persons waiting on the customers there.

"Take this in and ask Govind to check the value."

After a short while, the boy who was sent, came back with a slip and the gemstone and handed them to his boss.

"This is a rough diamond and needs cutting and polishing. You get ten thousands."

Vacra agreed to the price. He wanted some money badly to meet the expenses. He pocketed the money and left the shop without putting his signature in a register as required by him.

He then called a taxi and reached his hotel room. During his sojourn through Mumbai, he came to know that big jewelers-shops were located in East Malad.

Next day he proceeded to Malad and stopped in front of a big shop. He was informed that always big shops only were reliable. So he wanted to check his previous days experience with another shop, no harm that to be a big shop.

Vacra entered the spacious air-conditioned premises of the jewelers shop.

The girl at the glass covered counter in the first segment smiled and asked him about his requirement.

Then he was directed to the first floor. There he was asked to go to the hall at right end where only a few people attended to work. When he went in, he saw another closed glass shuttered hall, where many people were busily working on a number of small machines, some cutting diamonds and some others fabricating jewelry-items.

Vacra looked himself in the large mirror opposite to his seat. He looked sophisticated and different from the way he looked like in his earlier occupation.

A young man in his early thirties, fair and effervescent, beaming a bright smile came and sat opposite to him. Vacra took out the small purse containing a few gemstones, he wanted to sell and handed over one piece to the person opposite to him.

The other person held it in his hand, looked it under the bright light kept on the counter near him, which he switched on now. After a few moments he kept it down and asked for other pieces. He checked the five gemstones brought by Vacra, likewise and selected two out of them.

“The natural finds are all not good, some of them about twenty percent are only good for cutting and could be passed on as diamonds. Others are flawed and discolored.”

He spent some more time on the others.

“Colorless topaz like this one and some such sapphires are passed on as diamonds. You must take care while buying diamonds.”

“Do you have facility for cutting and polishing?”

Vacra asked the other who appeared to be ready to pass on his knowledge.

He pointed out to the hall which Vacra already saw while entering the enclosure, where many apron clad men were working.

“There, we get them worked upon. Only a diamond cut properly, emits out light entering from the top, in all directions. That is an ideal cut.”

He further clarified.

“The price depends on ‘carats’ of weight, hardness measured on Mohs scale and luster.”

He then called someone by name and entrusted the two pieces keeping them in a small round box for checking their quality.

Vacra was offered tea.

After some time, the person sent with gemstones, brought back the box with gems.

“These two measured around five and if you are interested to pass on, you can accompany the boy to the ground floor.”

Vacra agreed to the proposal and followed the boy to the ground floor.

He was paid two hundred thousand rupees in cash as Vacra preferred cash to check. He had no other option and accepted the price offered. He could not counter the offer with any other bargain, because he did not know much about the gemstones.

Moreover he now wants to start some business and needs money. Anyway he was better equipped now with fragments of knowledge he gained in the process of selling the gemstones.

He had to keep faith in the shop fellow, as there was no other way for him now.

Later he may check with other shops and gain knowledge of diamonds and other gems.

* * *

During the stay of a few weeks in Mumbai, Vacra with his tactful way of dealing made friends with hotel manager where he stayed. In due course of time he managed to secure a double bed apartment in Bandra area. The high denomination currency notes he displayed played the trick. He opened a bank account now, which gave him a standing in society. The first thing he did after opening the bank account was to get a locker allotted to him. He then deposited the gems he was left with in the bank-locker.

After that he again went to the jewelry shop where on an earlier occasion, he exchanged for cash two of his gems. He met Gowtham Jain the talkative employee who gave him the first level knowledge of gemstones. He offered him lunch at a star hotel. He met him a few more times to make the relationship closer. With the knowledge and contacts of Jain, he could sell some more gems at higher prices.

With his increased contacts and money deposits, he now planned to become a businessman to give the riches he owned an authenticity.

Vacra became owner of a fancy goods shop.

He then, after two months, brought his wife and son to Mumbai.

With his knowledge and contacts he got now, he began disposing off some more gems at Surat on the advice of Jain.

Vacra used to visit his relatives at his native place now and then. During one of the visits he saw his assistant Saral on the road. He was well dressed though looking thin. He was ready to fall on his feet with uncontrolled joy after seeing his boss again unexpectedly. Vacra pulled him to his chest and embraced. That was a different and unexpected gesture on the part of his boss. Saral narrated his story—how he returned home after a great ordeal and without reaching the peak of the mountain. Because of generosity of his boss, he could pull on without work for two months. Vacra provided everyone of his followers enough to survive. That was the reason why they used to work for him without questioning.

He asked Saral to meet him at his house in the night for discussions and planning for future.

II

It was quite some time back that Vacra and his group were engaged in operation burglary. They were not in news these days. So for police it was an abandoned group. Vacra and his group were not on focus for the time being. That's why Saral could easily reach Vacra's house in the night. It was past ten o'clock. Being a small place town, was asleep by then. Except for barking dogs here and there, it was practically silent.

Vacra was waiting for Saral. They were closeted in the front room for long hours.

Eventually, Vacra gave a sheaf of currency notes to Saral and said "Reach the station by seven in the evening with the tickets."

Saral left him with a broad smile.

* * *

When Vacra reached the railway station, Saral was already there waiting for him. He waited for him away from the entrance, farther away where he could not be easily located by others. It had become a habit for him and also others of his group, to stay away from the prying eyes of law. He stood behind one of the concrete pillars on the platform, watching for the arrival of his boss.

When he saw Vacra, he did not run to meet him at once. He looked around to check whether anybody was watching his boss. Vacra however had changed very much and did not resemble his former self. After that making sure it was safe for them to meet, Saral approached him with a broad smile.

Vacra led him to the class I waiting room. They had tickets for A.C class with them. The train which goes to Mumbai direct from that place was scheduled only once in a week. Otherwise they would have to travel to Delhi to reach Mumbai from there.

The train for Mumbai arrived in time and the erstwhile burglars settled nicely in their A.C class seats.

Vacra gave an opportunity to Saral to taste the rich food and drinks available on the railway coach. Saral enjoyed the menu very much. After some time Vacra opened his flask of foreign liquor and they both enjoyed the special treat. Saral was all praise for his boss's kindness. The twisted accent of the language of the duo was foreign to their two co-passengers, who watched them in awe at their way of conversation and mannerisms.

After free chitchat in the joyous mood, with the effect of drinks and food, Vacra and Saral fell asleep having tired themselves to the point of boredom. They got bored to the extent of losing inclination to talk any further either for entertaining the other or self gratification. The air-conditioned compartment and the smell of fresh thick rugs and bed covers lulled them to contentment beyond their expectations and experience.

They slept like that for a few hours.

Suddenly without any notice, two uniformed railway police officers entered the compartment and switched on the lights. They were in uniform. One of them, the senior officer tapped on the shoulder of the person sleeping on the upper berth opposite to Vacra.

He said in a haughty tone, "We are on inspection. Please open your bags and suitcases."

The person in sleep woke up aghast, "What?"

He uttered that and got down at once. He opened the boxes and bags of his and also his companion sleeping down below, while shouting the other to wake up.

They found nothing.

"What are you looking for sir?"

He ventured to ask.

"There were complaints of drugs smuggling on this train."

Due to this disturbance, Vacra woke up.

Now it was the turn of him to open his bags. Vacra watched the inspector checking the suitcases and bags of him and also of Saral, who was fast asleep.

The officers finally left without any result. There were no apologies or formalities of departure. Vacra then put off the lights and the occupants resumed sleeping. He pulled over the comforter and covers in full length and closed his eyes.

Vacra was never a fast sleeper. That in fact helped him in many of his adventures and also in encounters with the police.

Now, he casually stole a look towards the opposite berth. That man was pulling back a broad comforter like sheet made of small pouches under his bed sheet. They appeared like packets of what the police officer said 'drugs.'

After setting them back concealed under his bed sheet, he lowered himself on the bed. He did not see Vacra watching him. Vacra noticed on the others face the usual smugness and confidence found in a thief after accomplishment.

Vacra smiled to himself and slipped to sleep, while planning next day's action with respect to the other person.

The beams of sunlight pierced through the window of the compartment and touched the face of Vacra, who was turning side to side, after the long sleep, comfortably ensconced in the thick folders of the rugs and soft pillows.

His co-travelers on the opposite berth were already awoke and hibernating on the lower berth. One of them opened the curtain on the window, which allowed the sunlight in. He at once let the curtain in place again, after watching outside.

Hushed sounds of coffee and tea vendors on the platform could be heard now.

Vacra saw his watch; it was seven. Saral was moving hither thither in his bed without getting up.

There was a tap on the half open door which was not shut as the four of them did not belong to one family group.

"Coffee, sir, hot coffee and tea."

It was the uniformed vendor of the pantry car.

Vacra came down to the lower berth and shook Saral awake, who stood up at once with a grin in obedience.

He sat down on the lower berth and slid the curtain aside to have light in through the blue glass shutter. The platform was crowded with travelling public and vendors moving hurriedly on various errands.

"Two coffees."

The fellow who was from opposite upper berth ordered. Vacra saw him clearly now. He appeared sophisticated and dressed well like a rich businessman. His partner was shorter to him but dressed like the former in costly branded shirts and pants.

Vacra now ordered two teas, as they were accustomed to tea drinking.

The boy poured tea and coffee in shining porcelain cups and handed them one after the other.

The boy left after collecting money.

Vacra looked at the opposite berth guys and laughed aloud while taking tea, as if someone cracked a joke.

"Dear Saral, do you know there were police in the compartment last night?"

Saral was surprised and afraid too at this information.

"I don't know that. Why did not you wake me up boss?"

"They have come for drug smugglers. We are not concerned with that, you know."

"What happened then boss?"

Saral asked him still not sure of the news.

Vacra looked at the taller guy in the opposite seat obliquely and said, "Nothing; nothing happened as they could not find anything in this compartment."

The taller man in the opposite seat, whom we may call 'D', first letter in the word 'Drugs', appeared nervous for a moment and sooner regained composure.

He assumed the posture of a rich business man once more.

Vacra's aim was different. He planned to tackle the drug peddler in a way to be of use to him later.

He said with a crooked smile, "The foolish policemen thought drugs would be transported like bangles in suitcases and bags. They don't know there are other more sophisticated methods."

'D' became shaky and moved in his seat uneasily.

Saral could not understand what his boss was talking. But he knew his boss as a thorough schemer and clever in his own way.

"Tell me boss if the police would find the drugs somewhere?"

"Why not, but they should come to me for that. I also know that they offer reward for such disclosures by anyone."

Saral became now avaricious, "Boss, please help me get that reward."

Vacra looked at D and then at the upper berth to make the point clear to him, while the latter watched him.

But D ignored him.

Vacra said again, "At the next station, my dear Saral, you will get the reward, because the drugs are here in this very compartment."

Saral was flabbergasted and he looked at the other two. He understood now why his boss was talking all the while about drugs.

D became furious now. He signaled his companion the shorter man, whom we may call 'R' for the second letter in the word 'drugs'.

R whipped out a knife from his undergarment and tried to put it at the throat of Vacra.

Saral moved in a flash and gave a hard punch on the back of R, which loosened the knife to the floor of the compartment. Vacra pulled out his revolver and aimed at D.

"No more tricks. If you behave well we will negotiate, okay?"

Vacra gave ultimatum.

D now understood the opponents.

He asked R to come back to his seat.

Vacra laughed away the matter, while Saral joined him.

He said, "I know the trouble spot. It is right there."

He pointed out to the upper berth, where D slept before.

D nodded with a serious face and opened his brief case.

He pulled out a bundle of currency notes of high denomination and stretched out his hand towards Vacra.

Vacra pushed latter's hand backwards and said, "I don't want money. I want to do business with you."

He smiled genially and jovially.

D was surprised at this proposal. He did not come across anybody so cool in such circumstances. The opponent was as cool as cucumber. He was proposing business in such a risky venture. What does that mean? Was he already in this business? Or it is that he wanted to reach the big fish to catch, being a police person or an informer?

D looked at Vacra steadily for a few moments. He did not appear to be a policeman by any standard. His looks gave out that he was a hard boiled somebody, may be thug, a smuggler or a thorough scoundrel by any measure. Yet he has no way out now. He could be managed by talking politely for now.

D now smiled for the first time after the incident. His companion R became composed now and watching the drama going on, his face looked furious though.

"What do you know about this business?" D asked Vacra.

There was a creaking sound of the door; someone peeped in and gone. He was a young man with a backpack.

R got up opened the door checked both sides and closed the door. He resumed his seat beside D.

Vacra looked into D's eyes straight and said, "In fact I don't know this business."

"Then what else? What kind of business you were familiar with?"

He wanted to know Vacra by making him talk.

Vacra looked at Saral and smiled.

He replied, "We were in the business of burgled jewelry and so on. We purchase such articles from anybody and sell. Right now we are in diamond business, uncut diamonds."

D said impatiently, "Okay, okay. That is interesting. Now I can guess why you look so."

"What do you mean by that? You watch your words."

Vacra said sternly.

D smiled now and asked, "Alright. Now, how do you want to do this business?"

Vacra thought over for a moment and replied "Okay. you assume we are an extension of your shop, business or whatever it is."

"If that is so, you come to my office. I have other businesses too. This is my card."

He passed on his visiting card to Vacra reluctantly.

Vacra after a while went out of the suite and talked to someone on cell phone.

"Yes, you check the address of the person, and let me know if it is okay or not."

He returned to his seat.

The train slowed down. Next stop was Poone.

D got up picked the bed sheet packed with drugs, neatly folded and set it in the suitcase.

"I have some urgent business here in Poone. You meet me later at your convenience."

He told Vacra wryly. He then looked at R and waved his hand at him.

He got down from the compartment as soon as the train stopped.

Vacra did not get a call from his accomplice yet. He suspected something foul, the way D escaped.

He touched Saral on the shoulder and signaled him to follow him. They too got down to the platform.

Vacra gave a bundle of currency notes from his valet to Saral and asked him to follow D, without being watched, to find his movements and address there. He gave his address card and asked him to meet him next day at Mumbai.

Saral at once left him.

Vacra saw R too getting down from the train and buying some eatables. The train stood there for some more time.

They got in as the signal for the departure was given.

* * *

Vacra reached Mumbai without any further encounters with R.

Next day Saral met him in the morning at his house.

He narrated his pursuit of D at Poone.

"Boss, I followed that man at some distance. He talked on phone to someone. When he went out of the station, one young guy came on motorbike. They talked for a few moments. Then he handed over the suitcase to that fellow, before I realized what happened. He called a taxi and got in. I too called a taxi and followed him. He went to a building in the township by name 'Shivavihar.' I could not do anything further, as he did not emerge even after half hour. I noted the address and left the place.

He gave the address slip to Vacra.

"Alright, that fellow his name is...."

He searched his pocket and pulled out the card given by D.

He continued, "His name is given here as 'Varun Das.' His address is here. That is his office address; that is in Bandra."

He again said, "Saral, he had gone from us. You could not help it. That young man escaped with the 'mall' on a motorbike. No one can do anything in those circumstances. Now we have some addresses. Let us see."

Then he laughed away the matter.

In the meantime, his servant boy brought tea and snacks. They both passed away time talking about past incidents.

Vacra asked Saral to meet him in the evening at his shop.

* * *

Vacra was sitting in one of the chairs outside his shop and whiling away time, watching the traffic and people passing in front of the shop.

Saral saw him there.

He appeared like an embodiment of virtues with a serene face and well set features. He wore a white shirt and blue striped pants.

Saral wondered how he could become so cruel, once his interests were crossed by anybody.

Vacra saw Saral and with a hearty laugh called him in. They both entered the ante room to the shop reserved for proprietor. The room was furnished with a medium sized table with drawers and four chairs. There was a cupboard on one corner and a sofa on the other side.

The shop was busy with customers attended to by a few salesmen. There was an older man sitting at the entrance beside the counters. He was collecting cash and directing the staff.

"Boss, do you think that man named Varun Das hoodwinked us."

"No, no, I got his address in the card enquired by one of my confidents. He told me that Varun Das has an establishment in Bandra. That is a jeweler shop. He has an office too, I was told. I called you here so that we go and check whether he could be contacted there. Incidentally, we could deal with him in diamonds. I told you about those diamonds before."

Saral said, "Yes, boss."

Then Saral called a taxi and they proceeded to Seth Varun Das.

It was six in the evening. The entire street on both sides was lined up with large buildings housing shops of fancy goods, jewelers, clothes and so on. In the higher floors, offices of commercial establishments were located. Everywhere Vacra saw people moving around and cars parked on both sides of the road.

Vacra and Saral reached seventh floor of 'Macanjee mall.' The office of Varun Das occupied one third of that floor. Half a dozen persons were working inside and were visible through the glass paned walls.

Vacra contacted the receptionist and gave her his card. He explained the purpose of the meeting as business in diamonds. His card showed his shop's address with contact number and all.

Vacra waited in the reception room for twenty minutes.

The receptionist told him that the Seth was busy with a group of businessmen from Vadodara. When they left, he was asked to go in. Vacra told Saral to wait there and he proceeded in side.

It was a medium sized room with accommodation for three visitors opposite to the Seth's chair and beyond that a sofa at one side of the room.

Vacra greeted the Seth.

Seth looked at Vacra and took a few moments to recognize him.

He then smiled with complete composure. He could escape the ruffian easily in the train.

"Take your seat," he asked the latter not showing even an iota of familiarity.

"Now tell me the purpose of your visit here?"

Vacra looked into the eyes of the Seth straight. He too did not want to mention the train incident. In fact that was beyond any use now. No proof of criminality of the latter was with him.

He said, "I am doing business in diamonds, uncut ones. I have my own shop of fancy goods here in Mumbai."

He wanted to come out clearly now.

"So....?"

The Seth stopped at that.

"If you are interested, I will proceed further."

"Yes, I would like to see the samples."

Vacra pulled out a case with a muslin cloth piece well set with a few samples of each category available with him. He pushed that towards the Seth.

The latter examined them carefully.

After a few moments, he said "I am interested in them. We will talk further and fix prices in a later meeting, when I will involve my assistant who is an expert in this."

Vacra took back the samples and said "I will call you and fix an appointment, if you like it. Or you may send me a message at your convenience."

Seth now said "By the way, if it is not confidential, I would like to know the source of supply and the quantity so as to plan my work."

"The source of supply, I will not be able to tell now, but the quantity of each type I could give you in our next meeting."

Vacra became sophisticated and felt proud of himself for his acumen in business negotiations.

He remembered Jain, who gave him much information on diamonds and discussions on business.

The meeting ended with that.

"Seth Varun Das is a notorious man. He was in the news for wrong reasons many times. Ganeshji, you must be watchful about him."

Jain told Vacra about the Seth. Vacra was known as Ganesh now in Mumbai.

Vacra said, "Don't worry, we know each other well. I don't think he would venture to deceive me."

Vacra took Jain along with him for his next meeting with the Seth.

The business profited Vacra as well as the Seth. It went on for two months. Then the stocks depleted. Vacra had to plan another trip to the lower parts of the 'mountain', where he accidentally came across the source of gemstones.

III

Vacra planned the trip carefully. It had to be in stages to camouflage the purpose of the visit. First he would visit the town where he sold his first diamond. In fact he duped the businessman. He would have to pass through that town, as it was on the way to the 'Mountain'.

He would change his attire; of course he was already a changed man from what he was once. He became a business-man from Mumbai. Now he would go there as a trekker of mountain. Of course, he would take Saral with him. Saral was a reliable assistant since many years. He knew his boss well and would not venture to double cross him. They would carry sufficient food and other accessories including equipment for self-defense.

* * *

After equipping themselves well as planned Vacra and Saral started on trip to the mountain once more. They traveled on train up to Shimla. Some rest was necessary after the arduous train journey, as it was not a safe guess that they would be able to rest in later stages. Money was no constraint now. They checked in a star hotel there and enjoyed the luxurious fare for one day.

Next day early in the morning with a small luggage of two backpacks one for each packed full with all requirements, they took a bus to the town of Chota Bareile in trekker suits. They kept their suitcases with clothes in the cloak room there. By midday they reached the place. They had afternoon snacks in a small restaurant there. While they were eating, one local person was watching Vacra keenly. He went away after eating.

Vacra paid the bill and they came out on the road. His next stage of journey was Ramgarh. In his earlier trek he came down from the mountain by the same route. He did not know any other route to reach the place of gemstones.

He walked to the bus stand followed by Saral. While they were waiting under a tree, for the bus, two rough looking guys came near them. They appeared like local goons. One of them, the taller fellow pushed Vacra aside and while he was trying to stay erect, the former snatched away the backpack from him. But Saral at once pounced on him and tried to recover the bag. The second goon gave a hard punch to Saral and threw him down to the ground. Vacra did not expect any such incidents in those places and he at once pulled out a small penknife which he always carries in his pants pocket. He did not hesitate to plunge the knife into the shoulder of the tall guy, who was shocked at the harsh reaction. The local goons were flourishing by the fear they could create in the people, by their reckless attacks on unarmed men. But they were not accustomed to inflict bloody injuries on their victims in the process. They were small time criminals. Saral now picked cue from his boss and gave a deep slash on the face of the second goon with his knife. After all it was not new to them, but they never expected that to happen in that remote town. With that the two ruffians nursing their wounds ran away.

Vacra now saw at the nearby cigarette kiosk, a known face which was none other than the jeweler whom he tricked in his previous trip to the town. The injured goons were running towards him. So it was now clear to Vacra that he only was behind the attack on them.

There were not many villagers around to watch the scene.

Vacra dusting his clothes and backpack boarded the bus arrived then, followed by Saral. He felt like laughing at the silly incident. He narrated the background for the attack on them to Saral with intermittent laughter. Saral felt satisfied with some action on his part too in the affair. He said he was itching for some such activity after these many months of inaction.

The bus moved on. The conductor in the bus meted out special attention to them, as they appeared rich and special with their costly attire and trekker-outfits. All other travelers were ordinary poor village folk only. He knew they could afford better transport, but they were here in the bus, only for trekking the mountain ranges. They need to get acclimatized before going on the expedition.

After travelling a number of hours, they reached Ramgarh. On the way the bus stopped at some village, where the bus driver had tea and biscuits and smoked some cheap brand of cigarette. Vacra watched that, while smoking his foreign made cigarette after sipping perforce the tasteless village tea.

Vacra did not utter a word on the way. There was nothing new to talk about and moreover the subjects to be discussed were confidential to discuss in public.

Now it was trekking. No more automobile travels.

After getting down from the bus, they walked for an hour and stopped at a dhaba, a thatched roof hotel normally catering to the traveling truck drivers and also to occasional bus passengers. If the bus driver fancies stopping at the dhaba, he would get his food free whatever he eats. Of course all other passengers had to pay at the prevailing rates there.

The truck drivers going to far off places take rest on the string cots available there.

Vacra and Saral ate rotis and dal.

At the other end of the dhaba, Vacra saw two trekkers eating at a table. They appeared very hungry and heaps of food on plates was before them. Their shorts and other trekker's kits appeared much used indicating they were regular trekkers.

"My friend, I think we have company on the way."

Vacra pointed out those guys to Saral. He was a changed man now and did not mind calling his assistants as friends. Of course that was reserved for his erstwhile tested and trusted fellows.

"Boss, they could be going on a track they were familiar with; and it might not be our path."

"That is possible. Anyway we would have some adventure as you said you were itching for."

Vacra laughed loudly. However, it did not reach the ears of the competitive trekkers for good or bad.

After that they started on journey for the treasure trove, a known and tangible one, not like that supposed to be at the peak of mountain.

He led the way for Saral to follow. He had good memory and was able to go correctly by the land marks he kept in mind. However the trek up the hill was more taxing compared to the fall or trek down the terrain.

After a few hours, he had come to a confusing spot. There was to be a big boulder beside the sesame tree. The tree had fallen down across the path way and the boulder lied a few feet away from the tree. He had to wait there for finalizing the direction.

Vacra thought he would go some distance on the right side path to the boulder and look for next landmarks before going ahead further. It was not a pathway ready to trek on. But there was clear place enough for them to trudge on, between the wall like stone formations.

Later on, they could find landmarks like the burnt tree top and a cave like stone structure to confirm the correctness of the path they chose.

After a few minutes they heard voices partly in English and some Hindi. Vacra halted and looked on either side of the path, through the bushes and little trees. On keen observation, he saw the half pants fellows whom they encountered at the dhaba. He cautioned Saral not to make any sound. After a while the sounds of those trekkers became inaudible.

Vacra now was certain that the other fellows took a different route and had gone.

The confident treasure hunters were on their trek again.

The landscape changed now. The tall wall like boulders on either side appeared like guards appointed by celestial beings for guarding something ahead.

He knew now he was close to the gemstones.

The sun was descending on the west. Suddenly, there was a flood of light as that of a flash light focused on them. Saral stopped behind his boss at once and pulled out his knife ready to defend from some unknown, assumed intruder.

Vacra laughed aloud to the surprise of Saral and said "Nothing to be scared about. It is the reflected sunlight from the gemstones, my dear Saral."

He shouted in joy, "Jay Bhavani" in praise of Goddess.

Saral joined him, while putting back his knife in the sheath.

After a few steps, they saw the wall like boulder embedded with colored stones.

Saral could easily make out that they were not ordinary stones and must be of high value as the luster was unusual.

Vacra now said, "Saral, we have to pick out as many gems as possible. The bigger the gems the better and they are of our first preference. It is going to be dark in a few hours. It is now three o'clock."

Saral jubilantly said, "Yes, boss."

They were hungry after the continuous trek. Whatever food items they brought with them, they ate away at once. It was work now. Water was available at every stage of the journey, as small streams flowing down the rocks of the mountain. They quenched thirst with clear natural water..

They started picking out the gemstones from the clay covered walls on either side, with the instruments they brought with them.

They brought pouches suitable to store them. The pouches in turn were attached to a long broad sheet of cloth normally used to spread on ground to sit. Each pouch had zip closure to ensure its security. The gemstones were secured in the pouches. Vacra became methodical now, after his first trip to the mountain.

Vacra and Saral filled all the pouches with the gemstones and the bed cover like cloth sheets became heavy.

They emptied the backpacks of the things they brought like the rest of the food packets, instruments for plucking the gemstones and other accessories. They now stashed the cloth sheets with gems in the two backpacks.

There were many more gemstones on the wall like structures. They had no place to keep them and also they might not be able to carry beyond some weight.

They kept the knives and revolver only on their bodies now. The thick apparel was a must, however as it was very cold there already.

Vacra said they should discard the instruments which they would not be able to carry with them now. But the instruments should not be available to any chance trekkers to make their job easy. That would undo their future replenishments. So he advised Saral that those should be thrown away on different directions from there.

There was some place left in the backpacks after putting the cloth sheets. Saral asked his boss, why not fill them with some more gemstones. Of course the limiting factor was their capacity to carry the materials.

At last loaded in full they started on their return trek.

The trek down was dangerous in that unless they were cautious one slip may cost the life. But, as it was downward journey, the weight they feel was less, compared to the uphill task.

As long as they were between the wall-like structures, they could be easy on their care. But once they crossed that, the path was with a gorge on one side and the sharp rocky surface on other and they began trekking with more care. So the speed of descent became less.

The surroundings became colder now. After trekking down further it would be warmer at the lower regions.

The strain of trekking weighed them down and it was doubled with the anxiety to take care of the valuables.

The sunlight no more helped them. Vacra switched on the torch light.

After a while, Vacra fell forward when his foot hit a stone protrusion on the path. Saral helped him to get up.

He had to keep his backpack down on the ground before that. Both were strained but the enthusiasm of better lives in future only gave them strength to sustain.

They reached Ramgarh at last with bruised bodies and torn clothes. Time was eight. It was clear to them that they could not travel any more even on a motor vehicle that night. They wanted to rest. Of course taking food was a prerequisite.

Vacra asked Saral to look for a restaurant or any place in that village where someone was prepared to give them food for a price.

They put their backpacks down on the side of the road where they reached now.

There was a street light ahead of them emitting very low light on the surroundings. Half the village was already asleep.

A tea-shop fellow was getting ready to close his establishment for the day. Saral went to him and asked for food. Very reluctantly he agreed to provide them rotis and dal after taking some time for preparation.

The trekkers had no option but to wait. Vacra knew that no other source was there for food and shelter in that small village, particularly at that time of night.

The vendor of tea asked them to come in. They finished eating quickly as they were very hungry.

After awhile, Vacra asked shopkeeper whether they could sleep on those benches which were there for sitting and keeping food items.

The shopkeeper Raman looked at Vacra. They had already kept their backpacks on the benches and were relaxing.

The travellers appeared very tired and bruised. He saw occasionally tired trekkers of the mountain coming to his shop.

He felt pity looking at them.

He said, "Alright. You can sleep on these benches. But I cannot provide you with any beds."

Vacra replied with relief, "That's enough for us. We could adjust with these benches."

"But make sure you get up early in the morning before I get ready for the customers."

"No problem. We will wake up early. In fact we have to catch the first bus to Bareily tomorrow."

Vacra paid him two hundred rupees at once. He agreed to pay one more installment next day before leaving. He knew those shopkeepers might not have seen big money before and hence to keep him happy he would better pay well.

By the early rays of sun, Vacra and Saral were sipping tea given by Raman, the tea-shop owner. They woke up much before that and washed to the extent they could at the well in the backyard to the shop. They did this in turns, as one of them had to be on watch for the merchandise in the backpacks kept on the benches. It was merchandise truly as the gemstones were material for sale thenceforth.

Vacra paid the balance due to Raman and with backpacks on, they trod on to the bus stop which was close by.

They got into the first bus towards Chota Bareile. The conductor in the bus was the same person who traveled with them the previous day to that village. He was surprised to see the weather beaten figures of the two trekkers, who were recipients of his respect in the previous trip. He did not pay any attention to Vacra though he paid over and above the fare, in rounded off figures.

After getting down at Bareile, Vacra followed by Saral went to the cloakroom, where they deposited their suitcases the previous day after changing into track suites. At one corner of the bus stand, now they changed into clean clothes and kept the backpacks in the suitcases. It was twelve in the noon. They have to reach Shimla by night to catch the train to Mumbai at ten.

Vacra hired a taxicab at the taxi stand located next to the place where they got down from the bus.

While they settled at a star hotel at Shimla, a different situation that was detrimental to the future of Vacra was unfolding at the village of Ramgarh.

IV

Raman's wife Madhu cleaned up the benches and floor of the tea-shop, after the departure of Vacra and Saral. She found below one of the benches where the trekkers slept, an odd shaped stone of the size of a marble that village boys play on the street. To have a better look of that stone she took it to the light near the front door. It dazzled her eyes. She did not want to throw it away as it appeared like a gemstone though an ordinary pebble. She kept it on the desk where her husband collects cash at the front door. She thought it must have fallen down from the dresses or bags of those trekkers, having stuck to them on way down the mountain.

During the course of the day, customers while paying bills pick it up to have a closure look out of curiosity. Raman told its history to the first few. Later on he ignored the queries about the odd looking shining stone piece.

While closing the shop late in the evening, Raman found it more attractive in the electric lights. As each customer picked it in his hands for having a closure look, it lost its dirt covering, and became something like a polished one. Raman though liked it and kept it on the table, he doubted that it might be snatched away by somebody or more likely by a playful urchin. At first he had put it in the drawers of the table there but later on he changed his mind to take it home.

Raman lived in a thatched house at the back of his tea-shop or some called it restaurant too as some times food was also served there. Tea and snacks was the normal fare available. Occasionally long distance travelers and trekkers got food if they asked for.

At bed time, the subject of the shining stone came up while chatting about the days incidents in the village. Madhu asked for it to check it's luminosity as described by her husband. She got up from bed and picked it from the cupboard. After switching on the light she looked at it closely. She found it different from what she saw in the morning. Raman said it became brighter as the customers handled it day long out of curiosity. He then smiled and added jocularly that he thought it might be stolen by someone taking it as a gemstone. That's the reason he brought it home. In fact what he joked about he believed in his heart to be true to some extent.

Madhu after hearing what he said went to bathroom and cleaned it with soap and rubbed it clean and dry by a piece of cloth. Now it had shone like a gemstone. She remembered the necklace her neighbor showed her the previous day. She told Madhu that her husband gave it as a birth day present.

Madhu now sneered, "If I cannot get a real diamond necklace like my neighbor, let me have this put in my gold chain."

Raman turned to the other side and pretended sleeping.

* * *

Next day in the evening the couple went to the jeweler shop in the village.

The jeweler rubbed the stone with a piece of rough cloth and cleaned it with water.

He then asked Raman, "What do you want to do with this?"

Madhu replied while showing the gold chain she brought, "I want that stone put like a locket in this chain. Is it possible?"

She was feeling shy as the stone was not real gemstone. In fact she expected the jeweler making fun of them, to have brought ordinary stone to be put in a gold chain.

But the jeweler did not.

The jeweler then asked Raman, “Where did you get this? This would appear big in this chain. I would put a suitable diamond instead of this.”

Raman said, “I don’t have money for a diamond. That is why I brought this.”

“You need not pay me anything. Leave this stone to me. I will give the chain with a diamond to you after a week days.” Then he pushed a box with small diamonds on the desk towards them.

Raman understood by now why the jeweler did not jeer him for bringing a stone to him and why he would give a diamond free of cost. The stone piece they brought must be of some value or even high value.

He asked the latter, “What would be its value in rupees?”

“May be a thousand; anyhow unless I got it polished it would not be purchased by anyone.”

“Suppose I get that polished. How much would you offer?”

“You cannot do that. I know a diamond jeweler from whom I can get the work done.”

Madhu was happy with the offer of a cost free diamond. She already selected one piece of diamond from box and showed it to the jeweler.

She nudged her husband with her elbow and told the jeweler “Alright, I am satisfied with this one. Please do the job nicely.”

The jeweler smiled and said, while keeping the gemstone they brought in the drawer, "Please meet me after a week. The chain will be ready with this diamond."

Now he kept the gold chain in the desk and smiled again.

Raman was not fully satisfied with the price, but he could not do anything else in those circumstances. He got up and left the jeweler, wife following.

*　　　*　　　*

After a week days, Madhu received the gold chain well-polished and a diamond set in it.

In the afternoon, she called Sarala her neighbor over the border wall and showed her the shining gold chain. Sarala appreciated the gold chain and the diamond embedded in it.

The news of the gold chain with diamond worn by Madhu, wife of Raman made the rounds in the village. In no time it reached the money lender Sankar Lal, whom Raman owed a few thousands of Rupees and was not repaying the installments regularly. The loan was made when Raman improved his tea-shop. Having learnt that Raman could buy a diamond chain to her wife, he was miffed and went to him for repayment. As Raman had no money, he forcefully took over the chain.

On the advice of his friends, Raman reported the matter to the local police. Then the story about the gemstone and how they were given the diamond free in exchange came to light.

On enquiry the police got information that the jeweler could earn fifty thousands on selling the gemstone.

In course of time, the police at Chota Bareile, recovered the gemstone as it became the property of government; of course mined gemstones belong to the government.

Ramgarh police took note that the duo of trekkers who visited the tea-shop dropped it there by oversight. But they could not track from where they came there.

The case came to a standstill at that stage.

V

Vacra made a call to his friend Jain, asking him to meet him at his new office. Jain had become his advisor now. He had been paying Jain handsome amounts of money in exchange for his services, since he began business with Seth Varun Das.

Vacra bought an office accommodation near Central Station, where the glamour and glitch of big businesses would not touch his affairs, which he thought require more confidentiality. With that acquisition of new asset he had spent almost all his returns on gems.

The Seth was paying at the rates at which they started business deals over a year back. Vacra knew he was being exploited, because of the anonymity of the source of supply.

Jain came into the office. Vacra was alone in his chamber, but for the receptionist in the front office. The glass enclosure which separates them was sound proof.

"Please take your seat." Vacra welcomed his advisor.

"Is there anything urgent?"

Jain came during the business hours. It was eleven in the morning.

"Yes, the Seth refused to increase the rate even after all these many transactions. He is taking advantage of the situation. I knew he is paying me very less to what he gets on each deal. So I want to explore another agency similar to him. I mean without any trouble to me."

Jain never interfered in his dealings. He was contented and accepted whatever was offered by Vacra. He understood Vacra well and happy with him.

He replied, “Yes, Ganeshji, I knew he was not fair to you. I will certainly find out a person who is better. I have someone in mind that is trustworthy and wants long term association.”

“However, I cannot cut off with Varun Das at once. It may be harmful to my business. So I would deal with both parties for some time and stop business with the Seth later.”

“That is perfectly alright. You could inform him at that time that the supply is exhausted.”

“So, when do you want me to call you?”

“I will call you after discussing with some suitable persons and we can then decide about the person.”

Vacra thanked him for the visit and Jain left.

* * *

After three days Vacra and Jain took a train to Ahmadabad.

They met Rajesh Modi a tax consultant in his office on Patel Road.

“Mr. Jain told me about your requirement. Mr. Ganesh, I am confident that I could fix a businessman suitable to your necessity. I am in the business of accounting and taxation and I have contacts with persons in different businesses. I will act as a middleman between you and the other man. My dealings would be open. You would not lose on your profits because of my margin.”

He then stopped and again resumed after a moment of thinking as if the other person asked for a clarification.

“In case you want to deal with the person directly I will offer my services as a consultant. So you can decide and tell me.”

He had put the options before Vacra to choose.

Vacra wanted to discuss with Jain privately and with Mr. Modi's consent went to the balcony with him.

Vacra said, "Mr. Jain, I think in my type of business it is better to have less number of contacts. I don't mind how this man introduces the business to the buyers. So it is safer to deal with Modi only. He could be like a buffer between the buyer and me."

Jain smiled and said, "I also have the same view. We could let Mr. Modi deal with that business man on our behalf. We may not get a better price even if we deal directly because of our compulsions. Moreover this man Mr. Modi has experience with government agencies too, as he is a tax consultant. That might be an added advantage."

They then finalized the methods of contact and supplies and financial terms with Mr. Modi. He however did not disclose about his business with Seth Varun Das, as that would not affect this business.

* * *

As Vacra was in need of money to meet his household expenses and also for his business transactions, he began disposing of the gemstone stock at a faster rate. Moreover as he had to keep his business deals intact for two buyers, the stocks began dwindling. Even though he shifted a part of the supplies to Mr. Modi, the supplies to the Seth were to continue at least to some extent. As he gets more profit on dealings with Mr. Modi, his supplies to the former were more.

The business in diamonds was not like other commodities. The demand would be more on festival days and family celebrations. Rest of the time the business would be less.

Vacra involved Saral in transporting the gems to the two locations.

Vacra's son, Rahul was grown up now. He was a youth of twenty years and doing Bachelor's degree in commerce. That was one of the reasons for Vacra's necessity for more money. The price rise in consumables as also in assets was having a choking effect on middle class families. Of course Vacra's life style too changed now. The stocks of gemstones Vacra brought in his second trip loaded in two back packs were not many as to last indefinitely. After cleaning and cutting each supply did not bring him expected and fair amounts, as the Seth was paying at low rates.

Due to these problems, Vacra had to pressurize Seth Varun Das, to raise the prices as per the market rates. He was perturbed at losses he suffered due to the low prices offered by Seth compared to those of Mr. Modi.

So in due course of time, the supplies to Seth were reduced. And at last he stopped supplying to him anymore. He gave the reason that his stocks were exhausted.

But Seth Varun Das had a nagging feeling that Vacra's source of supply was free of cost to him. That was why he was reluctant to raise the prices. He could not get a reply from Vacra about the source of supply, even after questioning him many a time.

Vacra continued his supplies to Mr. Modi even after he stopped to deal with the Seth.

* * *

Seth Varun Das was trying his best to unravel the secrecy of the source of supply to Vacra. He attempted to corrupt Saral many times for this information, but failed. Seth's son Gaurav and Rahul were in the same college. He asked his son to get this information from Rahul by some means. But Rahul was ignorant about his father's business details. He only used to be available in the fancy shop when it was necessary. More than that, he was never involved in his father's business affairs.

Mr. Modi informed Vacra or Ganeshji as he was known to him, that his buyers wanted uncut gemstones of three months supplies urgently at once as he secured an order for gems from Europe. This export order fetches foreign exchange in euros which the businessman could use for import of some goods required by a local customer. Mr. Modi said that he was asked not to reveal these details as Vacra might be tempted to raise the prices in future transactions.

He said, however he bargained for a ten percent increase in price as the advantage gained by the buyer was much more. So it boiled down to the fact that the supply of a quarter of a year was needed at once, if Vacra wanted to have the advantage of rise in price. In fact Mr. Modi advised Vacra that he would pressurize the buyer to retain the price rise for future supplies too.

Vacra knew that the supplies would last only for six months more. But he could not miss the opportunity of rise in prices for future. So he agreed to the demand of quarter's supply at once for export. Saral was assigned the job of transportation. As usual he personally delivered the goods to Mr. Modi.

Mr. Modi later informed Vacra that the buyer agreed to retain the increase in prices for future supplies too. He was happy for the outcome.

VI

The police inspector at the Ramgarh police station was transferred before the usual term of three years. One of the reasons was that he could not solve the mystery of the gemstone mining. The transferred inspector Baburao hailed from the western region. He was not liked by the local people, as he was always thinking of getting a transfer back to his home town or district. The new incumbent was awaited eagerly, as the head constable who was in charge inspector, was equally lethargic.

At last an inspector by name R.S. Dhaniram was posted there. He was a young man of thirty years. From the day one itself, he began concentrating on the law and order problems there. He restored order by putting the local goons in jail. They used to indulge in small time crimes which were a headache to the local people. Of course there were no big robberies either from the surrounding regions or from the distant thugs. The people there consisted of mainly farmers and small traders. The tribal lot depended on the forest produce. So, big gangsters had no interest in those parts.

Inspector Dhaniram came from far north and he was disciplined and work minded. He earned a good name for himself and also for his staff in a short time. There was much talk among people about the trying conditions in which he worked before and the laurels he received. His staff followed in his footsteps as he did not allow cases pending indefinitely and corruption. The traders were happy to have got rid of the local goons as also the monthly mamools, amounts payable to police and other small inspecting officials.

Now, the inspector was assigned the task of finding the gemstone thieves. It became certain in higher strata of police that the gemstone found with the tea-shop owner Raman was only a tip of the iceberg. There must be large quantities of such gemstones or even bigger pieces valued at lakhs of rupees lying in mines somewhere near Ramgarh. The two trekkers must have carried away many such valuable gemstones, out of which one piece accidentally fell in tea-shop.

So inspector Dhaniram was in receipt of a reminder from his boss to expedite investigation in that case.

He started enquiry with the obvious first step, where the story began. That was the tea-shop of Raman.

Inspector asked Raman, "Do you remember from where the trekkers came to your restaurant?"

Raman liked the term restaurant used for his tea-shop.

He was all smiles.

"What is the matter? You are so happy about something."

Then inspector questioned him in seriousness. He did not like taking things easy while the questioning was going on.

Head constable intervened and said with a suppressed smile, "He liked you terming his tea-shop as restaurant. He is happy and could not suppress it."

The inspector then laughed off the matter.

"Okay, tell me now, where from those trekkers came on that evening?"

"Sir, they were in trekker's suites with backpacks. I don't know from where they came. But we always see many such people going for trekking on the mountain."

"What was in the backpacks?"

"I don't know that sir. But they appeared to be heavy and they took extra care about their belongings."

"How do you know that?"

"One person always used to be with backpacks kept on the bench in the tea-shop, while the other went out for attending to nature's calls or for washing himself at the well in the backyard."

"From here where they went? Did you ask them?"

"They came around eight in the evening of that day and left by early morning bus next day. I had not asked them, to which place they were going."

"Which bus plies at that time in the morning?"

"Sir, first bus goes to Chota Bareile. Now I remember, he said he had to catch the bus to Bareile. The buses that ply toward far off places only start at that time."

With that the questioning came to an end. The narration was recorded by the writer Nanak Singh, who was one of the senior constables. He was a Sikh and that could be made out by his attire of turban and all that.

"Nanak Singh, these trekkers who come here, go which side of the mountain. Can we track the route by which these trekkers go up?"

The inspector asked the writer.

"I have not gone closure to the mountain, sir. There is a temple near the base of the mountain. I go to that Gurudwara sometimes."

"Can you find out any other source who can give some information about that?"

"The cowherd boys go up the mountain, for grazing their cattle. They may be able to give information about those routes."

The inspector smiled and said "Alright, let us go there and find out what we could gather from them."

The inspector, Nanak Singh and another constable went in a jeep to the base of the mountain. A narrow path led the police jeep to the Gurudwara, temple of Sikhs and that path continued for a few miles further. Thereafter it was only a rough footpath not suitable for motor vehicles. A number of foot tracks led up the mountain in various directions from there. The police party took one of the routes and proceeded further by walk.

After a while they heard some voices and presently saw cowherd boys grazing their cows and goats.

When they saw the police personnel, those village urchins ran away in different directions.

The inspector said to the constable "Sardarji, without the help of the villagers we cannot trace the trekker's paths. We will return later to the place of Gurudwara and the village nearby to get some information."

They walked back to the jeep and later reached the village nearby. That was a hamlet of Ramgarh.

On the advice of the senior constable, he sent word to the village head to come there. They might get some information from the village head.

The village head paid respects to the inspector and stood near the jeep.

The inspector said to him, "We are in search of the path by which the trekkers go up the mountain."

"Sir, either you can go western side, that is where you went now or the opposite side. After going some distance you have to choose one of the many tracks from there to go up the mountain."

"Some time back, that was three months back, a couple of trekkers came for trekking. Can you get some information on which route they went?"

"In this season, many people go trekking. But I think correct information could be given by the cowherd boys. They move around those paths every day with their cattle. If you want I will go with you and talk to them."

It was already evening and the inspector had to attend to his office work.

He said to the village head man, "Govardhan, we will come again after two days. By that time you try to find out the information and we will continue further."

The police jeep moved away.

*　　　*　　　*

Next day in the morning the village head Govardhan went to the police-thana of Ramgarh.

He went there to complain about the missing cow of one of the villagers.

After making sure that the complaint was recorded, he asked the constable that he wanted to meet the inspector.

"In what connection you want to meet the inspector? He is busy now and would not like to be disturbed."

"He wanted me to get some information about the trekkers."

The constable informed the inspector about Govardhan and later asked him to go into the room of inspector.

The inspector was busy writing on some files. Govardhan paid respects and stood at a distance from the table where the inspector was working.

He smiled and asked Govardhan, “Tell me, what information you could gather about the trekkers?”

“Sir, about three months back, two trekkers passed through that way and the cowherd boys saw them. They could take us to that spot, where they were grazing the cattle. But they said they do not know from there where trekkers went. There were many footpaths from there to go up the mountain further. They also said on the same day two more trekkers went by that way.”

“That means we can go up to that spot correctly and beyond that it would be guessing and exploration only. I don’t know if I can spend time trekking on the mountains.”

For many more days the tracing of the mysterious trekkers remained elusive.

VII

Vacra was now left with one month's supply of gemstones only. He was busy in a way with the fancy shop and also with his investment plans. His taxation work was looked after by Mr. Modi who was a consultant in taxation and familiar with his business too. Mr. Modi asked him to be available at Mumbai in connection with the taxation work. Vacra had purchased some plots in the gated community of a company floated by his business associates. They were to be registered now. He could get a share in the business in their next venture, his associates promised him.

Keeping all this in mind, he was postponing his visit to Ramgarh for procuring the gemstones.

He discussed with Saral about the alternative plan of sending his son Rahul with Saral to Ramgarh. Saral was not very confident of managing things by himself. He was not sure of his capacity to do things without his boss by his side. Vacra wanted Saral to work independently and just to push forward. He said he would meet them at Chota Bareile on the third day. That means Rahul and Saral would wait for him at the hotel where they would stay on that day. He further said that if he could not meet them there, he would certainly meet them at Ramgarh bus stand or on the mountain track.

Vacra gave all the details. Saral had been assured of his boss' presence at the place of gemstones and thereafter. Problem could arise only at that point.

Vacra gave instructions to his son Rahul how to behave throughout the journey. He gave graphic details of the journey ahead of them. He gave directions how to move himself at every stage of the travel. He was specifically told not to talk to strangers and not to give details of themselves, family or journey. Thus Rahul could now understand the nature of the work assigned to them and the reason to be secretive about that.

Rahul already knew how to treat his 'uncle' Saral that was how he addressed him. He would not misbehave with him as he had been associated with him since childhood. He had been watching how his father treated Saral and how much he depended on him.

Rahul naturally felt the same regard and love as Saral expressed towards his family.

On the day of the journey, Vacra gave his unlicensed revolver to Saral. Saral felt honored with that gesture though that was offered to him as part of the precautions of the journey.

Saral knew how and from whom Vacra procured that firearm long back during their erstwhile vocation. Vacra told Saral never to give that to Rahul. He was provided with a penknife to defend himself in case of any emergency against animals or humans.

Saral and Rahul travelled by train to Shimla. After reaching Shimla, they stayed in a different hotel, but not the place where Vacra and Saral stayed before. They changed their names for reservation of tickets and thereafter. They procured fake identity cards at Mumbai before starting on this venture.

* * *

Seth Varun Das was peeved about the way Ganeshji, as Vacra was known to him, stopped the supply of gemstones to him. He came to know later, that Ganeshji was sending his supplies to Ahmadabad. No purpose would be served by knowing the name of the buyer there. Obvious reason for diverting the supplies, he knew was the prices. Ganeshji, however never insisted on increasing the prices. He would have considered that, if he did so. Now he was put to loss. He lost good chunk of his profits from this business.

He wanted to find out the source of gemstones supply to Ganeshji at any cost. He had failed earlier to get that information.

Seth discussed about this with his advisor Pai, who knew all about his businesses.

They then decided that, when Ganeshji goes for his next replenishment, they must send someone to follow him without being noticed and find out that place.

Seth fixed two of his reliable assistants on this job. They would make acquaintance with the workers of the fancy shop of Ganeshji and his house and find out when he goes on tour.

At last one of the assistants Pratheek came to know that Ganeshji was going on tour to an unknown destination, unknown to even his wife. He was going to some distant place in the north with his assistant Saral.

Seth prepared Pratheek ready for any travel at short notice, to follow Ganeshji. Through the workers at fancy shop Pratheek came to know the date of travel. Seth asked Pratheek to watch carefully and bring the information of the places they visited. He would do that without being noticed.

* * *

On the day of journey, Pratheek reached V.T. railway station following Saral and Rahul at a distance. He waited to find out Vacra, before they started for the station, but could not trace him with Saral. At last he followed Saral and Rahul, who proceeded to the station in a taxi. Pratheek knew Rahul as the son of Ganeshji, as he was watching them at their shop.

After reaching the railway station, he found them on the platform where the train for Shimla was standing. He bought a ticket in the sleeper coach, bribing the ticket collector and boarded the train. He saw Saral and Rahul getting into an A.C. sleeper coach. When the train started he made a call to Seth informing him that Saral and Rahul were going in Shimla train and that he was following them. He also told him about the absence of Vacra with them.

Pratheek did not see the duo on the platform later even though the train stopped at some stations. They got down at Shimla and Pratheek too alighted hastily so as not to miss them.

At Shimla, Saral and Rahul hired a taxi and reached a star hotel. Pratheek too went in a taxi to that hotel following them. He informed the Seth about possible higher expenditure because of the lavish lives of the target duo. Seth did not mind about the expenses involved. He wanted to find the location of the source of the gemstones. So he asked Pratheek to gather the details of that at any cost.

Rahul enjoyed the trip. He was never allowed to go without his parents tagged on to him.

Saral was like a friend and he liked his company. He enjoyed the good food and drinks too. Saral could not stop Rahul after all he was son of his boss. He was enjoying small pleasures for once. And money was no problem now.

They stayed overnight there and waited for Vacra. Next day, after lunch, Saral made a call to Vacra. He said he was busy and could not come to Shimla. He asked them to go over to Chota Bareile and stay there for that night. He told Saral to stay at a different hotel, but not the same one where they were on previous trip. He advised him to avoid leaving any trails of their presence there.

Saral and Rahul proceeded to the bus-stand and waited for the bus going to Chota Bareili after changing into trekking suits and backpacks, having already kept the suitcases in cloakroom with their luggage of two suitcases.

Pratheek saw the target duo at the lunch time and was aware of their preparation to vacate the room. As he had to avoid them, he waited for his turn to clear the bills and vacate his room.

When he came out of the hotel, he saw his target duo going off in a taxi car. He noted the taxi number. He at once called a taxi man and told him he missed his friends, who went before him. He asked the driver of the taxi to take him to his friends and he gave the number of that taxi car. The driver told Pratheek that car went to the bus stand and that he could take him there in no time. Pratheek offered higher fare if he took him to his friends.

Pratheek feared he might have missed the duo and with a pounding heart he reached the bus stand. Luckily for him the target duo was seen waiting at the bus bay. He thanked God and then made a call to his boss giving him information up to that point. He told him he would make a call afterwards as he did not know where they were bound to.

Pratheek was noticed by Saral when he got down from the taxi and hurriedly moving with his bag to the bus lobby. He remembered to have seen him somewhere at Mumbai but could not connect him to any location.

When the Bareile bus came, the duo hurriedly got in. Pratheek too boarded the bus taking care not to be noticed by the duo.

During the course of the journey, bus stopped at a place for the passenger's tea and snacks and other needs. Rahul and Saral had tea and snacks.

Rahul went to the toilet to ease, while smoking a cigarette. He picked up the habit in the college. Then he saw Pratheek looking at him. When the eyes met, the other turned away quickly as if he did a mistake.

When the bus stopped finally at Bareile, the duo took an auto rickshaw and reached a lodge. Saral chose a different lodge avoiding that he and boss stayed before.

Pratheek followed them at a distance and however went to the same hotel. He could not locate any other lodge nearby.

So they all stayed at the same hotel and Pratheek gave the information to his boss.

Saral received a call on his cell phone from Vacra asking them to move on to Ramgarh by the first morning bus. He said he would meet them there. He asked them not to make any phone calls to him and that he would inform them of his plans and also give directions if needed.

By the time Pratheek woke up next morning, the occupants of the target room vacated the room and gone away. The receptionist of the lodge could not give any information as to where they had gone.

Pratheek cursing himself for his laziness vacated the room. He enquired with the room boy as a last chance of getting some clue. The room boy said they had gone to the bus stand which was close by.

Pratheek with his bag on his back ran to the bus stand at once.

When the target duo was boarding the bus to Ramgarh, he ran after the bus and could get in at last.

Saral saw him getting into the bus. Now he began doubting that person, as he appeared to be following them from Shimla or might be even from Mumbai as he remembered to have seen him there.

Saral and Rahul sat in the second row behind the driver.

Pratheek was in the last row at the end of the bus.

Rahul said, "Uncle, I saw one person following us from Bareile. He might be following us even before."

Saral smiled and said, "Yes, I agree with you. That person boarded this bus and sitting in the last row now. I doubt that fellow and guess I must have seen him somewhere at Mumbai."

"Why he is following us? Do you think he is a policeman?"

"I cannot say, I will talk to boss after getting down at Ramgarh. We could judge him further from his behavior then."

Rahul looked back and saw that person looking out of the window in the last row.

One row away behind them on a seat next to the window, another person was watching Saral keenly. Saral was known to him when he accompanied Vacra during their previous trip. He was the jeweler who was duped by

Vacra during his first visit to Ramgarh. He tried to avenge his loss last time but failed.

As soon as the bus stopped at Ramgarh, Pratheek who was in the last row got down from the exit door there. He took care now not to lose sight of them, without being seen by them.

Saral and Rahul with the backpacks intact alighted from the bus and walked over to a tea-shop near the busstand.

Saral called Vacra after making some distance from the crowd.

"Boss, I saw a person, a young man of thirty following us from Bareile, I have a doubt that I saw him even at Mumbai somewhere."

Vacra replied "You watch him now. You try to avoid him before going to the mountain. I don't know who he could be; may be a policeman or someone acting against our interests."

"Boss, are you not coming here?"

"Saral, you can manage it. Rahul is there for any help. I am stuck up with the work here."

Saral guessed from the beginning that his boss might not come this time.

He smiled and said "Okay Boss, we will manage it."

The duo entered the tea-shop and had tea and biscuits. Saral ordered for meal and waited for it.

Before going up the mountain they should eat food and also carry something packed as there won't be any source of eatables later.

When Saral looked out of the window, the suspected person was not seen anywhere outside.

VIII

The jeweler who traveled in the same bus as that of Rahul and Saral came to Ramgarh to meet his sister. But having seen Saral, he changed his mind and wanted to get even with the trickster's group.

After getting down from the bus at Ramgarh, he went to Raman's tea-shop, which was opposite to that where Saral and Rahul were waiting for their meal.

At the time of paying bill, he pointed out Saral, who was sitting in the shop opposite, to Raman and told him how that man's friend cheated him. The jeweler told him that Saral who was Vacra's associate now came with another person. They both had backpacks on them and wore trekker's dresses.

Raman recognized Saral as the person who came with Vacra to his tea-shop a few months back and wanted by police. He told the jeweler about that incident and asked him to stay quiet as the police would take action. He then sent word to the police inspector about the arrival of Saral, one of the trekkers wanted by police, to the village.

The jeweler heaved a sigh of relief for the news and now had his tea and snacks with relish. He was not a man of greed and never thought beyond his loss. Any other person would have thought of the gemstone affair more seriously and benefited some way. He was satisfied with justice to his hurt pride.

* * *

Inspector Dhaniram when he got information about the arrival of one of the gemstone thieves in the village, left all other work aside and readied to follow him to the spot of the mines. He told the informant to keep an eye on those visitors.

He alerted the constables to be ready when required. He started with Nanak Singh at once towards Raman's tea-shop on bicycles without wearing uniform.

As an afterthought, he asked two constables to go over to the place near Gurudwara with the jeep and wait for his message.

Saral and Rahul after picking the food packets moved fast towards the mountain. There was no trace of the suspected person anywhere around that place. They thought either that person was not harmful or he must be hiding to follow them again without being observed.

Pratheek took care not to be seen and followed them at a distance. As they were going by walk, chances of missing them now were remote, he thought.

Inspector Dhaniram with his assistant followed them keeping sufficient distance between them and at the same time not losing sight of them. He wanted to follow them incognito till the place of gemstones was reached.

After some distance, the inspector was surprised to notice another person following the visitors. Pratheek followed them in advance to the police and he did not notice them.

The drama went on till Saral and Rahul reached the place where the cowherd boys were seen by the police last time.

The target duo looked around to make sure that nobody was nearby. They picked the route to the place of gemstones and were on their trek further.

Saral said, “Rahul, I don’t know what happened to that person who was after us. I hope he is not following us anymore.”

Rahul replied, “Uncle, we cannot rule out his presence still. He might be following us more carefully.”

It was already twelve but the sun was not hot. Saral asked Rahul to hasten his pace so as to reach the place of gemstones early. He knew after five it would tend to become dark. They must reach the place and must be able to pick as many gemstones as possible in that short period. They decided, in case the suspected person was seen, to eliminate him so that the secret of the source would remain with them forever.

After an hour, Pratheek slowed down and rested on a boulder beside the path. He thought he could rest a while and follow them. He knew he would not miss them as the pathway was narrow and there was no other way to go for target duo.

By this time after one curve in the path, the policemen came in sight of Pratheek. He saw them and thought some other visitors were on their way and might not be connected to the duo.

So he did not move or hide from them. Inspector Dhaniram went near him and put him in conversation.

“Is there any village nearby?’

“I don’t know. I am going on some other work and I am also new to this place.”

“Where are you going? You don’t appear to be from this place.”

“That is none of your business. Leave me alone.”

So saying Pratheek who became angry with the interference to his work got up from the boulder and walked on.

The inspector stopped him by holding his upper arms tightly. He then asked Nanakram to put handcuffs to him. He at once called the constables waiting for his orders at Gurudwara, to go over there. He ordered Nanakram to proceed on his trek to follow the gemstone thieves.

He then asked the handcuffed Pratheek, "We are police personnel. Now tell me who are you? And why you are following those two trekkers?"

Pratheek was already very much tired due to the unusual strain of journey and secretive work. He was shaken to the core when he heard of police. He did not expect that he would have to face police in this work. His boss too did not give him even a clue about the possibility of police in this affair.

"Yes, why are you keeping silent? Tell me everything. You will be saved if you are without any fault."

Pratheek wanted to save himself.

He said, "Sir, I will talk to my boss and tell you."

The inspector permitted him. He thought there was more to this than simple theft of gemstones.

However before that, he asked him, "Who is your boss and where does he live?"

Pratheek gave the visiting card with the name and address of his boss on that.

He then called his boss and told him about his arrest by the police and requested his help for returning to Mumbai.

Seth understood that he was in trouble because of his miscalculation of the affair of following Vacra. He denied anything to do with it and asked his assistant to take care of himself.

When the police called him too, he did not agree with anything his assistant told them.

After sometime the constables reached the inspector. He asked one of them to take Pratheek with him to the jeep waiting at Gurudwara, to be lodged in custody later.

The inspector and the other constable again were on trek to reach the duo of thieves.

Saral found the place of gemstones as it was seen by him last. Walls on both sides of the path were glistening with gemstones. Without wasting any time, they hurried to pick them one by one, giving priority to the larger ones.

After one hour of trekking, Nanak Singh could trace the duo of gemstone thieves, as they were referred to. He saw them ahead of him. Afterwards they stopped in between the wall like stone formations. He saw the shining stones on both of the wall formations. They were like shining stars when the sunlight fell on the walls.

Nanak Singh wondered the way how the duo picked the gemstones from the walls and neatly packed them in cloth pockets. He was surprised to see how prepared they were ready with the instruments and backpacks with them. He continued to wait for his boss.

The inspector took time to reach that place as he was waiting for the constables and sending the arrested Pratheek back.

After going further, Nanak Singh spotted his boss and colleague trekking carefree. They did not know they were close to the target place. As there was a curved pathway at that juncture, the gemstone thieves did not notice the intruders.

Nanak Singh hid behind a huge rock tried to catch the attention of his boss, by making low sounds.

The inspector did not catch the hints and they proceeded on.

When they turned the curved pathway, Saral saw them. He thought them to be some passersby going that way missing their route. Yet it was risky to give away the clue to the gemstones. He cautioned Rahul at once and they hurled stones at them to scare them away.

At that point of time, Nanak Singh called the inspector to come back to safety.

Saral now heard the voice of another intruder and guessed there were many out there.

He shouted to Rahul to be cautious and the necessity of hiding from them.

The police persons now became visible to them. One of them, the constable though in plain clothes was holding a police stick. Saral could make out that they were policemen.

He said in undertone about that to Rahul.

Rahul as he was inexperienced with such adventures became nervous and he was also angry as they could not complete their work. He snatched the revolver from the pocket of Saral and fired without proper aim.

The sound of the firearm reverberated through the rocks.

The inspector having come to know that they had a firearm cautioned his colleagues and opened fire at the person who fired at them.

Immediately a deep cry of pain and thud was heard. Rahul was hit on the chest and he fell aside. Saral was never in charge of any operation before. He too feared of the repercussions of this attack. But as a first step he took Rahul in his arms and tried to stop the blood oozing out of the wound with a cloth piece immersed in water.

He shouted in anguish to the policemen that his colleague was in danger and asked for help.

The inspector saw the duo of thieves and understood that the game was over. He knew they were a group of two persons only and one of them is shot. He ordered Saral to put his hands up after putting the revolver on the ground.

Saral did as ordered by the inspector. He was hand cuffed.

The inspector asked his men to help the injured man. A phone call by the inspector brought a doctor of the local hospital to the place where the police jeep stopped. The injured man was carried down by the two constables, Nanak Singh and another, as fast as the terrain permitted.

The inspector R.S. Dhaniram made another call for two more constables to reach that place along with the village head at once. He had to make the gemstones mine secure.

When Saral who was in the custody of the inspector now, came close to him, he was shocked to identify him as one of their former co-trekkers Ramasaran.

He blurted out, "You are Ramsaran, what are you doing here?"

With a smile Ramsaran Dhaniram, the inspector said "Yes, I am Ramsaran. I have become inspector of police after my studies back home."

On their trek down, he narrated how he survived the fall after Vacra tried to kill him and with persistent efforts how he has become a police officer.

Then he asked, "Where is your boss Vacra?"

Saral gave the details of his part of the story.

EPILOGUE

The doctors could not save Rahul. The delay in carrying down the injured over the mountain terrain to the hospital resulted in loss, blood and medical aid could not be given to him in time. A shocked and depressed Saral sent the message to Vacra with help of police.

Inspector Dhaniram informed the mines department regarding the discovery of the gemstones mine in the lower parts of the Green Mountain near Ramgarh. After three days the mines department took over and took measures to make it secure.

The dragnet of police spread wide and they took action against the beneficiaries of the gemstones starting with Vacra then Seth Varun Das and Mr. Modi and the buyers from him. Vacra lost his son and the fortune he earned by illegal means.

ABOUT THE AUTHOR

V. Hanumantharao, is a Cost and Management accountant by profession and a writer by passion. He has worked with the Government of India for some part of his life and later started his own consulting firm. He was also involved in teaching and had taught management students.

He has been writing short stories and novels from 2002 and this is his fourth novel.

Some of them are on Amazon.

Short stories on Amazon.

1. Mystery Unfolded.
2. The Family Affairs.